Gerald Beresford Fitzgerald

Clare Strong

A Novel. Vol. 1

Gerald Beresford Fitzgerald

Clare Strong
A Novel. Vol. 1

ISBN/EAN: 9783337066024

Printed in Europe, USA, Canada, Australia, Japan

Cover: Foto ©Andreas Hilbeck / pixelio.de

More available books at **www.hansebooks.com**

BY

G. BERESFORD FITZGERALD, *F.S.A.*,

AUTHOR OF 'LILIAN,' ETC.

' La meilleure Philosophie relativement au monde est d'allier à son égard
le sarcasme de la gâieté avec l'indulgence du mépris.'

CHAMFORT.

IN TWO VOLUMES.

VOL. I.

LONDON
F. V. WHITE & CO.
31 SOUTHAMPTON STREET, STRAND, W.C.

1889

PREFACE.

———

Every human life, if faithfully told, has probably an interest of its own, and a moral, perhaps, for those who come after, journeying painfully across an arid waste and finding few oases. Anyhow, it seemed to me that the life of Clare Strong had as much human interest in it as many biographies which I have recently perused, after first having heard their praises sounded.

To give lists of the guests at your

dinner-table for a series of years, and of those you met at other people's houses, and to spice their conversation with Joe Miller's, at which Methuselah may have smiled rather faintly in his nine hundredth year, may be biography, but fails in the human interest which is the one thing needful.

One fact I must add, namely, that the dates at which this autobiography were written are somewhat ambiguous. Clare Strong certainly wrote at long intervals, and it is impossible to say when he first commenced his story. Consequently, there are presumably gaps in point of time.

He died in a remarkable way. He

was living in his beloved Paris, where latterly he passed so much of his time, and, walking back with his wife from one of the *cafés* on the boulevards, where they had been breakfasting, he complained, on reaching their apartments in the Avenue d'Antin, of feeling unwell. She placed him on a sofa in his library, and flew to get some *Eau de Cologne.* When she returned to the room, his head had fallen on his chest, and all was over.

He thus realised his own constant prayer for sudden death, and for death not at an inn, as Sterne's somewhat artificial aspiration went, but without a long and lingering illness, without a deathbed struggle, and weeping relatives, and paid attendants to swell the scene.

But he was not buried as he once expressed a desire to be, in the Greenwood Cemetery, overlooking New York, but in the quiet graveyard at Carnaby, near those whom he had so dearly loved in life, where the roses in the long summer days still bloom luxuriantly over his tomb, and over that of his beloved, though far more distinguished, friend, ' The Right Honourable William Penrose.'

' Requiescant in pace.'

THE EDITOR.

CONTENTS.

CLARE STRONG.

CHAPTER I.

ANTECEDENTS.

'Conceit you me.'

I WAS born considerably more than half
a century ago, in Upper Grosvenor Street.
I often pass the house, and gaze, as one
is apt to do at houses one once knew
well; but the shutters seem always put
up in the drawing-rooms, and the brilliant parties which in my youth issued
therefrom have long since passed into
the land of shadows. Who was it said,

after living a lifetime in London, that the town became a city of the dead,— that is, of dead memories?

I was born under one great disadvantage, and I think it the greatest conceivable. My mother, judging from her pictures, a very lovely young woman, died at my birth, and I was her only child. My father, who was in the 3d Guards (now the Scots Guards), was always extremely delicate, and the loss of his wife, to whom he was tenderly attached, affected his health to such an extent that the symptoms of that fatal decline to which so many of his family had succumbed, began to show themselves. He only outlived his young wife two years, and thus, at two years old, I was left to the care of his mother —my grandmother—in whose house in

Upper Grosvenor Street I had been born.

Before, however, speaking more particularly of my grandmother, who so largely controlled my somewhat chequered destiny, I should like to say how much reason I have to regard my poor father's memory with affection and interest. For it is clear, from the few papers and letters I possess of his, including his last testamentary injunctions, that he was a most loveable and delightful man. I cannot help quoting, in support of this, a clause in his will, which provides for the comfort of his horses after his death, and also a reference to one or two of his regimental friends. He is buried in the little cemetery in the Bayswater Road, where he was taken from Grosvenor Street. I was too young to know how my grandmother was affected

by the death of this her only son ; but I
fear the love of the world had even then
eaten away her heart, and that she was
not capable of any intense grief.

Here are the extracts I refer to :—

' I leave to Colonel B. the sword given
to me by His Royal Highness. I trust
he will do me the favour of wearing it for
my sake, and I am quite sure it cannot be
put into better hands. To Captain V. I
leave my large silver snuff-box. It is a
testimony of affection from a brother officer
and an old school-fellow. I leave to C. C.
S. my chestnut horse " Agamemnon," and
hope he will not sell him, but, when he can
no longer do his work with comfort, send
him over to M. to pass the remainder of
his days in rest and quiet. I desire that
my old bay horse " Brownrigg " may be
sent to M., and turned out there ; and it

is my *particular* desire that he never again
be ridden, driven, or do any kind of work ;
and I likewise desire that, from the be-
ginning of the month of October until the
month of April, he may have two feeds of
corn each day. I likewise desire that the
farrier may occasionally come over to see
that he is in health, and that his feet are
in good order. My reason for specifying
all this (however ridiculous it may appear)
is that I wish the old horse to be quite
comfortable, for he has been to me a most
faithful servant. To Her Royal Highness
I leave my little grey pony, and my bay
mare " Fidget." '

My grandmother was a Frenchwoman,
of Huguenot extraction, and her maiden
name was Chamier. She inherited a large
fortune from her father and his brother,
who, having migrated from France first to

Holland and subsequently to London, had amassed great wealth in the City. When she married my grandfather, Clare Strong, she was no longer young, and had refused many offers of marriage, as she very frequently, in later years, informed me. In fact, I believe she was thirty-eight years of age, whereas my grandfather was a professionless young man of twenty-five. Nevertheless, she outlived him, and also, as already said, the only issue of the marriage.

As it was impossible for her to continue her dinners and 'routs,' as they were then called, without a male assistant, and as I was only three years old at the time, and I could not be made use of, she married Sir Everard Duncan, of an old Lincolnshire family, and connected with every one whose society she at all affected.

Sir Everard was a very simple, good-natured old man, of a school which hardly exists now. He was extremely polite to my grandmother, who received his distant attentions with the coquetry of her youth, and he looked most dignified and imposing at the bottom of her dining-table, where, though he said but little, and that little of an uncompromising character, he was generally voted an excellent host, and a good old fellow.

London society fifty years ago was, it need not be said, very different in every respect from what it is now. To begin with, the Americans had not then crossed the Atlantic, to descend, like Byron's Assyrian, on the Dowagers' fold. The German Jew element of London society was, of course, not then in existence, and the men who had an influence in the world, were men of undoubted birth and breeding, whose antecedents were matters of history. One can scarcely realise what the feelings of the *grandes dames* of that day would have been, for instance, at reading the paragraphs in the papers of to-day describing parties, and ladies' dresses and jewels. But their surprise would not have been greater than when they read the names of the ladies who wore the dresses and the jewels, and even wrote the description for their own advertisement. These names were unknown in Mayfair in those days, and it would be unkind to say more than that.

Lady Duncan was connected with the City by parentage, and even had City cousins, whom she had long ignored; but her family were noble in France, and she was herself, in both manner, and appearance, and mind, of the *ancien régime*. Her husband, too (who was always a most kind step-grandfather to me, and who left me several thousand pounds), was a rigid Tory, to whom birth and breeding were in those days synonymous terms. Lady Duncan was one of those persons who seem to outlive everybody, and I have often wished she had outlived me. A very good digestion, and no conscience, are excellent things in life, as cynics tell us. Well, my grandmother had the former, and I don't think—in later life, at all events—she troubled herself much about right and wrong. How easily I seem to see her now, after so many years, walking on Sunday morning to her church in North Audley Street! One of her footmen, a few paces behind, with her large

red morocco prayer-book, followed leisurely
her mincing steps; for she was a little
woman, and latterly much bent.   She
went to church always without fail every
Sunday morning, and as regularly devoted
herself to the scandal and gossip of the
London world with her numerous visitors
in the afternoon.   I am told that this, too,
is a thing of the past, since cigarettes,
and curacoa, and coffee take the place of
afternoon church.   .

But the other day, glancing over some
letters of my grandfather's, I came upon
one written to him by my grandmother
before their marriage, and apparently while
their engagement was not countenanced,
which places her character in a better
light, and which is such a contrast to the
modern epistle written under similar circumstances, that I transcribe it in full.

But I beg young ladies—if I am ever so fortunate as to find any of them readers of these pages—not to sneer at a style which, in some respects, appears to me to bear favourable comparison with specimens I possess (not, of course, addressed to myself) of a more recent date.

'How unfortunate a being is your Marie, obliged to deny herself to the very person who most on earth she wished to see! Indeed, my most amiable, such was my very cruel situation on Saturday even. My poor, dear mother — for I still sincerely love her, notwithstanding her perverseness in condemning me to a situation and society highly disagreeable—has been indisposed with an intermittent fever, which returns every other day. Saturday was her bad day, and she had had a very

severe attack. I was sitting by her bedside when your carriage drove to the door,
and, though my heart whispered me it
might be you, I had not power to retract
the orders I had given of a general denial,
as my friend Mrs V— and her little girl,
who are with me on a visit, were at that
very instant in the front parlour. Under
such circumstances as these, can you forgive me? Indeed you cannot conceive
the uneasiness it has given me. I wrote
you a few lines on Sunday even, but was
prevented sending them, having no opportunity of conveying them to the post.
This morning is the very first that I have
had. My mother is, thank God! much
better. To-morrow is her well day. Per-
mit me to add we are disengaged, and
shall be at home the whole even. I dare
not say more. However, should my most

amiable be better engaged, or not disposed
to favour me again so soon, let me entreat
him to oblige me with a few lines, as an
assurance of that forgiveness, for which I
remain, his very humble and affectionate
suppliant, MARIE CHAMIER.

'Wednesday Morn, 8 o'clock.

'*P.S.*—I should not have mentioned our
being disengaged to-morrow even, but as
Mrs V. is with us, we are frequently out
of an even, and I should be extremely
sorry to subject you to a second disagreeable jaunt.'

It is melancholy to reflect that the Marie
Chamier who wrote this charming letter,
even when no longer young and perhaps
versed in such matters, grew into a worldly,
cynical, old woman, whose one idea was
gaiety and society, even when she had

passed her eightieth year. I do not believe she ever wrote or spoke to her second husband, Sir Everard, in such a submissive strain, nor did I ever hear her address him as my 'most amiable.' But we all change as the years go by, as much morally and intellectually as we do physically, and I am afraid I take the pessimist view that we do not, as a rule, change for the better. Youth is best with its golden aspirations, its summer dreams, its fierce and delusive passions, its boundless possibilities, and its impulsive folly. If I had known my grandmother in her youth, I dare say I should not hold the opinion I have long held of her character. Unluckily, I knew her in her extreme old age.

Sir Everard died when I was sixteen, and a boy at Eton. He was always extremely kind and generous to me, and I

felt acutely the news, which was brought
to me by my grandmother's old butler,
with whom I returned to Grosvenor Street,
to attend the funeral. It was my first
personal contact, since I grew up, with
death, and it impressed me accordingly.
After the funeral—which took place in the
old graveyard, long since closed, where my
father is buried — there was a heavy
luncheon in the dining-room in Grosvenor
Street, where I had to take the head of the
table. I had always been treated with considerable deference by my grandmother's
friends ; but now my consideration seemed
increased as I suppose, because the death
of Sir Everard left me the only heir. But
I recollect being much shocked at over-
hearing, unintentionally, a nephew of Sir
Everard remark—no doubt disappointed
at the contents of the will, which left the

bulk of his property to my grandmother absolutely,—'You will see she will marry again.'

I did not see my grandmother that day, as her maid informed me she was not well enough to do so, but she sent me her love, and would see me the next day. I afterwards discovered she had been closeted the whole afternoon with the said maid, examining certain large boxes of mourning clothes. But the next morning, after breakfast, as she knew I had to return to Eton, she sent for me, and received me in the most correct mourning of the period, which certainly was not so becoming as that adopted by disconsolate widows of the present day. She looked, poor woman, very old and wrinkled; and her bay wig, and broad velvet band across her forehead, could not conceal her great age. She kissed me very affectionately, and at once plunged, with her strong practical good sense, in *medias res*.

'I have always wished, Clare,' she said, 'that you should go into your father's regiment, and dear Sir Everard wished it too. He has now added to the capital your father left you, which has been carefully nursed, so that when you come of age, though very far from rich, you will be able to live in the regiment, and I shall hope to supplement your income. The late Duke of N. put your name down long ago, when you were a baby, for a commission, and we shall be able to advance the money out of your capital; and I think another six months at Eton will complete your education, so far as school is concerned. Then, Clare, begins your education in the world, and I hope you will commence it here, and take care of me.'

She spoke as if a long life was before her, and with quite a cheerful interest in the career of a boy who, in those days, was slim, lively, and good-looking. What could I do but kiss her, and tell her I would do everything she wished? She gave me a five-pound note, and her fingers to kiss, and I took my way to Windsor that evening well content with the world and its prospects, so far as I was concerned.

CHAPTER II.

NOUS NE SOMMES PAS D'ACCORD.

'Voulez vous voir à quel point chaque état de la société corrompt les hommes? Examinez ce qu'ils
sont quand ils en ont éprouve plus longtemps
l'influence—c'est-a-dire dans la vieillesse.

My grandmother retired for the space of
one long decorous year,—not abroad, as
ladies under similar circumstances do now-
a-days, but to her little property in Kent,
which she had bought in the early days
of her first widowhood, and where my
father had spent his youth. Her amusement there was the constant devouring of
the most romantic French novels; and
when I joined her there in my summer
holidays, I often found her in actual tears

over the sorrows and disappointments described therein ; and yet I do not think she ever shed a tear for any real distress. Perhaps she never met with it. Anyhow, as soon as she came back from her daily drive, out came the last French novel, and after dinner, having no parties to go to, she usually fell asleep.

This was not a gay life for an Etonian of nearly seventeen. But I was of a studious turn, and finding a few books in the house, and having a horse to ride through very pretty country, I got on fairly well. My grandmother was a great letter-writer in those days, even when franks were necessary, and her worldly friends kept her *au courant* of all the scandals and gaieties of the great world. She used to come down to our very simple dinner, I recollect, covered with her diamonds, and lean-

ing on an ebony stick. I once ventured
to say to her,—

'You pay me a great compliment,
Granny, in wearing all those jewels when
we are only dining *tête-à-tête.*'

She made a little odd bow which was
very French.

'I should have no opportunity of wearing them, *mon cher*, if I reserved them
now for society.'

When I went back to Eton for my last
term, she showed me a letter from a very
illustrious personage with whom she was
on intimate terms, assuring me of my commission ; and remarking on the complimentary manner in which my poor father was
referred to, said,—

'We shall spend next season together in
Grosvenor Street.'

I do not think she ever realised how

very different my views of life were rapidly becoming from those she had planned for me. As a middle-aged man now, I think the schemes of the elders for the young are generally doomed to failure, and that a better course is to let a young man follow his own bent, if he has the means and the opportunity of doing so. Some characters resent dictation on these matters; and it does not at all follow that because a father has been a soldier, his son has inherited the military instinct. He has presumably had a mother, and may have inherited some characteristics from her. Of my mother, Lady Duncan never spoke to me. I now know they could never have been friends, and I also can very easily guess why. My great ambition at this period, hitherto totally ungratified, was to travel; and the books within my reach on travels were eagerly read by me, and only served to stimulate my curiosity. I was also, in every sense, of a studious and contemplative turn of mind. To this day— having seen so much of men, and women, and countries as I have done—I cannot help feeling a sense of contempt, which I try to suppress, for the energetic fussers of the world,—for the people who boast they are never idle, and who rush from one pursuit to another. They are, after all, only post-boys; and the dust, and the clatter of the wheels, and the cracking of the whip, deceives the world for the time.

With these ideas, and, perhaps, to be candid, a slight bent of indolence, the career of a soldier, even if only an ornamental one, presented no attractions; and I felt—however disappointing it might be to my grandmother—the time was fast approaching when I must tell her that I had no intention of purchasing a commission in the Guards. I had so seldom opposed her in any transaction of my life, that I could form no idea how she would receive this resolution. But I feared a scene, and so, with true cowardice, after consulting with my greatest friend and contemporary at Eton, one William Penrose, I wrote the following diplomatic note,—

'ETON COLLEGE.

'MY DEAR GRANNY,—I think I ought to write and confide to you how very much I dislike the idea of going into the army as a profession. To begin with, I don't think I am at all suited for the life; and I would much rather wait for a time before deciding on my course of life. I would rather travel, and see the world, before I make up my mind on so serious a subject ; and I think my trustees would enable me to do this. I hope you won't be disappointed,—and remain your dutiful grandson,

'CLARE STRONG.'

What my grandmother's real feelings were on receiving this letter I never shall know ; but she only wrote to say that we could talk it over when we met. Our next meeting was in Grosvenor Street, when I had finally quitted school.

'My dear Clare, there are a few people dining here quite informally to-night. Two very old friends of mine, both military men, amongst them, who will talk after dinner to you about the Guards. They are both Guardsmen. One, Lord Francis Sherlock, you know,—one of my earliest

admirers, and who takes a great interest
in you. He asked me to marry him
many years ago, and he has never married, which makes my refusal of him
quite a tragedy.'

'I recollect him, Granny. I am not
surprised you never married him,' I
answered, somewhat drily.

My grandmother raised her eyeglass,
rather astonished, but went on imper-
turbably,—

'And the other—General Rosemere—
you know only by his fame.'

I really think Lady Duncan showed
a want of diplomacy in her treatment of
her grandson at this period. If she had
argued with me,—appealed to my father's
memory, and love of his regiment, and
finally fallen on me with tears and kisses,
I should probably have succumbed. But

to invite two ' old fossils,'—as I mentally
called them,—who knew nothing of my
character, or aspirations, to ' talk me over,'
was to invite failure. Lord Francis—of
whom there is much hereafter to be
related—was an old *roué*, who, over my
grandmother's excellent port, dilated, not
so much on the glory of his country, and
the smartness of his former regiment, as
on the necessity of a profession in first
starting in life, to keep a boy out of mischief, and on the obvious fact that the
only profession open to a gentleman was
the army, and the only regiments suitable
to a gentleman of means, the Guards.

' When I say " keep you out of mischief," of course, you'll get into mischief.
Every man of spirit has his day ; but
absolute idleness is very expensive, and is
apt to cripple a man.   You'll find Lon-

don very pleasant, as the young master
of this house; and you'll have your
friends elsewhere. Egad! Clare, I wish
I was you, and had your prospects.'

'My lord, I want to travel. Every
young fellow travels now-a-days before
he settles down.'

'You shall travel, when you march to
beat the French. We shall go at them
again some day, and then you will have
travelling enough.'

'Well, I am afraid I shall have to
disappoint my grandmother. I feel no
inclination to be a soldier,' I answered
doggedly.

Lord Francis was a man of pleasure,—
an old bachelor with an evil reputation,
and too little time left to him to argue
with a stripling. He turned abruptly
away, to discuss with General Rosemere

(the youngest cavalry general in the army)
the charms of some lady, about whom
both seemed to have much to relate. As
we all rose, Lord Francis said good-
naturedly to me,—

' You have scarcely begun your gallant-
ries yet. Take my advice, and steer clear
of very innocent enthusiastic ladies.'

General Rosemere laughed. In after
years I knew him well, as these pages
will relate. He was then also a bachelor;
but he lived to remember this advice,
thus addressed to one who did not in
the least comprehend its meaning, and
attributed it to the excellence of my
grandmother's port.

What passed that evening, or the next
morning, on the subject of my career,
between Lord Francis Sherlock and my
grandmother, I never knew; but, the

following evening, I escorted her to a
ball at her earnest request, and so far ac-
quitted myself to her satisfaction at my
first London party that, driving home as
wide awake as a girl of eighteen, she
said,—' My dear Clare, after all, the profession can wait. You will stay with me,
and go out this season, and pay visits
with me in the autumn, and we will see
later on.' She actually kissed me. I little
guessed then that her benevolence was
dictated by the fact that I had unwittingly
(sweet innocence of youth!) danced twice
with the greatest heiress in the room.

CHAPTER III.

CARNABY MANOR.

'Oh, thou oft depressed and lowly;
 All my fears are laid aside,
 If I but remember, only
  Such as these having lived and died.'

IF the atmosphere of Upper Grosvenor Street, and the society to be found there, was of 'the world worldly,' I often escaped into the country, to stay with the Penroses, mother and son, at Carnaby Manor. William Penrose and I had first been at a private school together, and afterwards entered Eton the same term, and we always remained fast and warm friends. His mother, the lady of the Manor at Carnaby, was one of the most remarkable

persons I have ever known. At her birth
all the fairies presided ; for she was born
an heiress, and subsequently inherited the
property at Carnaby, and the lovely old
Manor House, in which she lived, except
when in London in her house in Devonshire Place. Very rich, she had also been
exquisitely beautiful, and, even as an old
woman, the regularity of her features, and
the sweetness of her smile, and the expression of her large brown eyes, seemed
to win both old and young to her side.
She was also extremely clever, and a great
reader, and brilliant talker.   No wonder
that such a woman filled her houses, both
in London and the country, with the most
famous of the artistic and intellectual
world, who delighted in her society, often
dedicated their works to her, and enjoyed
the literary rest afforded them among the

beautiful gardens, avenues, and fish ponds of Carnaby Manor. Yet Mrs Penrose, with all her outward prosperity and success in life, was, in reality, a very sad woman. She had lost all her children, except William, and they had been six in number. One by one they were laid in the exquisite little churchyard in the park, and often, when no one was near, Mrs Penrose might have been seen among the rose trees, standing weeping over the graves where those she had so tenderly loved took their last rest. But she was too clever and too good to allow her own melancholy to affect her life, and that of those around her. Her village was a model one ; her church, which she had restored, was the most beautiful in the county ; and there was not a villager there who would not have gladly made any sacrifice for her sake, so dearly was she loved and respected. 'Her charity,' as was once finely said, 'knew no distinction save that of want.'

In many respects, William, my dear friend, had inherited his mother's fine qualities. He had her noble, impulsive nature, and the same expansive mind; but, perhaps naturally, he had not her strong literary tastes and instincts. He made but little use of the books with which the Manor House was stored—even the halls and passages were lined with books; and besides the fine library, there was a delightful bookroom filled with rare volumes, where many an entrancing literary work had first been written. William was a keen sportsman, and devoted his winter to hunting. He had the softest heart, and the warmest affections, of any man I have ever known; and his admiration for his mother was the ruling passion of his life. He often said to me,—'Was there ever anyone like my mother? She never thinks of anything but giving other people pleasure. I feel quite ashamed, sometimes, when I am with her, of my own selfishness.' And amidst this great love of the mother and the one child left to her, there was a constant humorous banter. Her poetical, romantic view of things was often to him a subject of great amusement. Her new mottoes, and the verses she placed on the tombs of her dogs and horses; the constant purchase of books of poems written by obscure and unknown authors,—all this he often rallied her about. To see them together was a charming spectacle; for he was as handsome as Apollo, and as simple and unconscious as a rustic virgin. 'My country friends,' as

Lady Duncan always called them, it may be imagined, afforded me a delightful respite just now from the endless, frivolous chatter and vapid gaiety which filled up my grandmother's life. At the very entry to the hall at Carnaby Manor I felt I was in an atmosphere congenial to my feelings,— where I could breathe, and think, and feel, —where I was sure of a sincere and genial welcome from its mistress, whose dulcet tones still ring on my grateful memory.

One lovely summer evening in July I had escaped from London for only a Sunday. The others who made up our party had wandered out among the flower-beds after dinner, and I found myself alone in the old bowling - green with Mrs Penrose, the full moon sadly sailing overhead, amid a silence which could be almost heard.

'I have always looked on you as Willy's brother, my dear boy,' she said, in answer to some words of mine of gratitude for her constant kindness, 'and as a son to me. I wish I saw your future marked out quite happily for you. But you will have most things the world wishes for, except, perhaps, distinction. I don't think, Clare, you are ambitious. But still there is much to be done in life without ambition, for oneself. What a good and merciful thing one knows not the path before us! and if we did, how many of us would ask, "Why were we born?"'

Her tone of profound melancholy was unusual.

'I suppose we shall know some day,' I said doubtfully, 'the whole truth.'

'"In that great day, when," as Addison says, "we shall all be contemporaries together." But whatever happens—and at the very worst moment of your life, dear Clare —remember to trust eternally and humbly in God. Quite a Sunday lecture,' she added brightly, as she saw I was thinking of what she said. 'And so you won't go into the Guards. Well, I wish Lady Duncan would consent to your travelling with Willy, as I presume he has told you he is most anxious to go to America— with a tutor, of course—for some months, and, I suppose, I shall have to consent.'

In those days, America meant a very long voyage, so Mrs Penrose's unselfishness did not seem at all to guarantee to me my grandmother's consent to a perilous journey. Besides, I knew she counted on my company both in London and the country visits she always made in the autumn.

'Granny seems to have forgotten all about her wish that I should enter the 3d Guards, and now seems to want me to be always with her. It is very flattering, but a little embarrassing.'

Mrs Penrose smiled.

'She is very old. Perhaps your first duty is to be with her. It is a marvellous comfort, in years to come, to think you did all you could in duties of that sort.'

Willy and I smoked until late into the night that evening in the wonderful old room devoted to that purpose at Carnaby, discussing our mutual love for travel, and the possibilities of ever seeing America, and going round the world. I found he rather agreed with his mother that I ought to remain as much as possible with my grandmother for the present.

'We will travel together some day,

dear boy; and I expect I shall be here
all the winter: I can't give up the hunting this next season.'

The turret bell tolled the small hours
as we boys talked our friendly and, perhaps, shallow philosophy.

The day came when I was to sit alone
and desolate, and to hear that bell, which
had a ghastly tone for me, as I listened for
the sound of a voice that was still for ever-
more.   But not yet,—not yet.   I went to
bed, and thought how, having no mother, I
was blessed to have such a friend as Mrs
Penrose.   At breakfast we were a jovial
party.   The lady of the manor was in her
happiest mood, and the grave portraits
of her ancestors and ancestresses in the
long dining-room seemed to me to beam
with satisfaction at the charm and gaiety
of their present representative.

CHAPTER IV.

A COMPROMISE.

'The Shape with " Thanatos " upon its brow,
   Dreadfully peeps.'

My return from Carnaby on this occasion
was memorable always to me, because my
grandmother, in her ever capricious way,
suddenly veered round, and suggested a
compromise as to my future.

' I have been thinking it all over, Clare,
and as you have such a decided distaste
to the army, why not go to Oxford,—to
Christ Church—and take your degree ?
You will spend your vacations with me,
and, after all, I can't expect to keep you
always here.'

I asked for a little time for reflection, and after communicating with Penrose, I told Lady Duncan, if the money question could be settled, I would gladly do my best to matriculate at Christ Church,—an effort which did not necessitate great labour in those days for an Etonian.

' I will consult the trustees, and we will have a meeting about it. I think you ought to be able to live on four hundred a year.'

The end of it all was I entered at Christ Church, and, to the great delight of his mother, Penrose also made up his mind to go up to Oxford too ; and so once more we were thrown together in daily intimate intercourse. I have no idea of describing myself, or my career at Oxford ; for it would be highly unprofitable reading,— neither new, nor interesting. I frankly confess—whether it was my own fault, or not—that Oxford did very little for me, and I look back on the three years which I was supposed to spend there, as very nearly, if not altogether, wasted. I went there a studious youth, and I remain a studious man, but not altogether in the collegiate sense, as study was then understood. The great variety of my reading was altogether against any academic success, and a translation from a famous passage in De Faublas, into Greek verse, was, as the old Scotchwoman said, on another occasion,—'Mair curious than edifying.' Nor can I say that I ever felt the sentiment about Oxford which, in common with most Etonians, I always shall feel about my school-days. I suppose I do not make friends easily. Those I made at Oxford I certainly can count on my

fingers, and they never did much in later life.
My grandmother's friends, of course, had
sons and grandsons at Christ Church, and
to her it seemed a constant annoyance
that I did not choose my friends in the
same worldly way she did, and had always
done, herself. I verily believe that her only
idea of 'the house' was a society where
opportunity was given to make friends
with men of rank and high social position.

The day before I took my degree, I
received a note which upset me very much.
It was from the old butler in Grosvenor
Street, to say that my grandmother had
had a bad fall, coming downstairs, and
would I come to London as soon as possible? Now, the note had been delayed
in coming to me, and it was already two
days old. Moreover, it was impossible
for me to leave Oxford until after the

morrow, nor was it possible for me to let them know in Grosvenor Street how I was situated. Penrose had failed to take his degree, and had gone down to Carnaby. There was no one whom I cared to consult as to what I ought to do. I arrived at, probably, the best conclusion,—that nothing was to be done except to wait until I could get away, and then start forthwith for London, sending a note at once, and taking the chance of whether it or I arrived first. As I drove up in a hack-carriage, I looked up at the windows; for my brain had been in an excited agitation for some days, and I had pictured the worst, and that I should find my grandmother very ill, perhaps dead. But all looked as usual as I rang the bell. Dorling opened the door, however, with a very grave face.

' She is better, sir, but she is very much

shook, and she has taken on dreadfully, sir, that you didn't come before. She is in the back drawing-room, as usual; but she looks altered somehow.'

I hastened upstairs, and opened the door of the smaller drawing-room. There sat my grandmother, dressed just as usual, and Mrs Dorling was reading her a letter. But she did not seem to notice my entry, and her eyes had a fixed, glassy expression. Otherwise, there was nothing in her appearance to indicate any change. I put out my hand, and she held it. I kissed her, and then she said rather weakly,—

'Why didn't you come before?'

'I couldn't, Granny. I took my degree yesterday.'

She seemed not to hear.

'Mind, Dorling, you take me to the

drawing-room windows to-night. I must see the people go in to the Duchess's party opposite. The house is to be illuminated. What a pity I cannot go myself!' Her voice was perfectly clear, though weak. 'I shall dine with you to-night, Clare;' and, leaning on her maid's arm, with difficulty she hobbled up the stairs to her bedroom. For years I had urged her to sleep on the drawing-room floor, where there was a boudoir, which most easily could have been converted into a sleeping-room. But her strength of will, derived from her Huguenot ances- try, had always opposed any supposition of failing health, or advancing years. It was most painful to see her going upstairs that evening, and to hear her say she meant to come down to dinner. I retired into the small sanctum downstairs which

had been mine ever since I had had a
room of my own, and rang the bell for
Dorling, who was my devoted friend and
ally, having often befriended me by sitting up when I had gone surreptitiously,
as a boy, to the play.

'This won't do at all, Dorling. Her
ladyship is far too ill to come down to
dinner. We ought to send for a doctor
who will forbid it.'

Dorling shook his head.

'If your grandmother means to do a
thing, sir, not all the doctors in Mayfair
will prevent it, as long as she has the
strength to do it.'

'But she hasn't the strength,' I retorted,
'Has she seen anyone to-day?'

'Lord Francis was here the whole
morning, and a young military gentleman
I never saw here before. I'm fearful, sir,

your grandmother has been adding a codicil to her will, and she isn't fit to make one.'

'Has Lord Francis been here every day lately?'

'Every day since the accident, and sometimes twice a day.'

'Will you ask Mrs Dorling to say to her ladyship how much I hope she won't attempt dining downstairs to-night; and that I should be so grateful if she would send for the family doctor, who would ensure her having a good night's rest.'

I then shut the door, and dressed myself for dinner, though my mind was greatly agitated as to what I ought to do on the old lady's behalf. In those days, people dined, when alone, at seven o'clock, and, at that hour, I found myself alone in the back drawing-room, so familiar to

me. There was my grandmother's green
parrot, chattering away in his usual shrill
way—the large worked screen, and the
miniatures on the tulip wood table beside it, the cushions she occasionally
stuffed—for she never knitted,—and the
oil painting of my father, which, as not
being a good work of art, never held a
place of honour in the large drawing-room.
I was glancing at it all—such a familiar
arrangement—once more, when I heard a
shuffling of steps on the passage outside,
and, hastening to the door, found Lady
Duncan descending the stairs to the
dining-room, with her maid and a footman
supporting each arm.

To my amazement, she was *en grande
tenue*, and her black satin dress was
covered with diamonds. I never saw a
more ghastly sight, and, as I followed her

down, I repeated to myself, 'O Iago, the pity of it!' She sank, almost breathless, into her large chair at the head of the table, and the dinner, which I have never forgotten, almost immediately began. After a glass or two of wine, and a little fish, she seemed, in some measure, to recover herself. But not a word did she ask me as to my degree or my journey, or anything personal to myself or to her. To the last she seemed full of the frivolity of her present life.

'It is the greatest disappointment to me, Clare. I had hoped to go to-night. But it is impossible. The Duchess never forgets her old friends, and knew I should enjoy such a beautiful spectacle. Three new beauties come out to-night, and all the Royal Family will be there who are in town. But I shall

see them go in from my bedroom
windows.'

She was fanning herself, and all the
time her poor face was twitching with a
sort of paralytic affection. Towards the
end of that terrible meal, when Dorling
was alone in the room, I made one last
effort, by saying,—

'Well, Granny, I hope they gave you
my message. I want you to let me send
for Sir William. He will just come in
from Brook Street, and give you a com-
posing draught, and to-morrow, I daresay,
you will feel quite yourself.'

She looked at me in a very fixed and
resolute manner.

' My dear Clare, I was never more myself than I am to-night. You will finish
your wine ; and will you ring for the servants to take me upstairs ? I am going

to my own room ; but not to bed. Go
to your club, *mon cher*, and enjoy yourself, and, if you're not too late, come and
say good-night.'

The Dorlings came in ; and I kissed
her wrinkled cheek.

' Don't sit up, dearest Granny ; I shall
say good-night now.'

' As you will,' and she returned my kiss.

I heard them labouring upstairs. But,
of course, I had no intention of leaving
the house that night. I went to bed at
eleven, and called Dorling before I did so.

' If my grandmother is worse, wake me
at once.'

He shook his head.

'She is at the window in her room,
watching the carriages and the company
going in.'

I was very tired, but it was long before

I fell asleep. The noise of the carriages, and the shouting of the linkmen, were sufficiently disturbing; but my thoughts were more so. I lay tossing on my bed, living, as fever patients do in their delirium, through all the scenes of their past lives. Every now and then, as I might have dropped off to sleep, the cries in the street awoke me, and I seemed to see, in a nightmare, the figure of my grandmother bidding me farewell, and fading from the room. I was within a few days of my birthday, when I came of age; but I think, in that night, like the man in 'The Spectator,' who put his head into the tub, I lived through a long life of horror and imagination. At last I woke with a sudden scare.

'Who are you? What is it?' I exclaimed, and my tongue seemed fever bound.

It was Mrs Dorling who was standing by my bedside, and had evidently, as gently as possible, aroused me. The sun was streaming in through the curtains, which she had partly drawn. The new day, and another of those thankless journeys for glittering Phœbus, had begun—but no new days for Lady Duncan.

'Oh, Master Clare, all is over! She died in her sleep, ten minutes ago, without a struggle; her breath grew weaker and weaker, and once I thought she smiled; but she never said a word, and I think she was asleep. I sat up with her all night, and she would not go to bed until late.'

What with my weird night, and my sudden awakening, and a possible general weakening of nerves (for I had been working hard) I broke down, and burst into

tears.   After all, I was very much alone.
We had not really had much sympathy ;
but she was the last link with my child-
hood, and all that the interests of early
boyhood mean.   And death is always
terrible to the young.

CHAPTER V.

MY GRANDMOTHER'S WILL.

'All heads must come
To the cold tomb ;
Only the actions of the just
Smell sweet, and blossom in the dust.'

In the present day, the shortness and uncertainty of life have become so impressed upon the minds of people, that they abridge, so far as possible, and in some instances totally dispense with, all outward sign of mourning for those of their kith who predecease them. 'I shall never be out of mourning if I put on black clothes for all my relatives who die,' I heard a lady once say, and I am bound to confess I found that very few of the

relatives who survived her made much
or long change in their toilette when *her*
death was announced.   But thirty years
ago etiquette was still observed in such
matters, — at least among persons who
came, like St Patrick, 'of dacent people ;'
and wills always, or very generally, contained provision for the mourning of
servants.   I observe in several wills of
the early part of the last century in my
possession, that, even to brothers and kinsmen, money was left to buy mourning ;
and, I suppose, cynicism might suggest
that such bequests betokened a doubt as
to the mourning being adopted, unless
prepaid.

As soon as I had dressed myself, I
wrote a note, which was immediately taken
by hand to Mr Bandon, the family lawyer,
asking him to come at once to Grosvenor

Street, and announcing my grandmother's
death. As my grandmother had never
alluded to her will, or to her death, or any
testamentary wishes, it was manifestly impossible for me, as her heir-at-law, to take
any steps whatever, without consultation
with him. I was sitting over a breakfast,
which I had hardly touched, when, to my
relief, he was announced. I had known
Mr Bandon all my life, and he had always
been a kind friend to me, although punc-
tilious in the old-fashioned solicitor's
manner of reserve and humility.

'Will you do what is necessary, Mr
Bandon, about the funeral, and all the
arrangements? You see, I have no experience in these matters, and I trust
everything to you.'

He seemed gratified at my confidence,
but, at the same time, a little puzzled.

'I must tell you, sir, Dorling stopped me on my way here, to say he had fears Lady Duncan had made a codicil to her will yesterday, and that she was not in a condition to have done so. Now it is impossible her ladyship could have done this, as the will was made ten years ago, and has always remained in our office. Probably Dorling has been talking nonsense. Still, he declares that Lady Duncan was busy writing yesterday morning, and that she sent for General Rosemere, and that, after his arrival here, a young Guardsman, whom he did not know by sight, also came. Altogether, though there may be nothing whatever in it, as a matter of form, let me have your grandmother's keys.'

I went upstairs to Mrs Dorling to get them. 'How little,' I thought, 'anyone seemed to feel for her death!—how selfish is the world!' I did not realise then, as I have years ago done, that, in the long run, the world is very fair in its valuation of its votaries, and wisely keeps its tears and charities for those who deserve them. The keys found, Mr Bandon proceeded very prosaically to open the old-fashioned drawers of the high escritoire at which my grandmother often wrote. She some-times wrote in her boudoir, I reminded him, as he tried the various keys, and sometimes in the small drawing-room. We were now in the dining-room.

'It will not take long, probably,' he said, 'as, if she executed any paper yesterday, it will be at the top of other papers.'

There had been a constant knocking at the front door since nine o'clock,—servants coming to inquire, and returning with hushed steps. But now Dorling entered, and asked if Mr Bandon would see General Rosemere for a moment. He glanced at me, and I saw, in spite of his effort at composure, that he feared trouble.

'I am very sorry. Say I am engaged with Mr Clare Strong, and can see nobody this morning.'

We heard the General depart, and Mr Bandon continued his search without result.

'I will ask Mrs Dorling where Lady Duncan was writing yesterday morning,' and he rang the bell.

It appeared from what Mrs Dorling said, that my grandmother had sat in the back drawing-room all the morning, and had received General Rossmere there. So we both went upstairs, and the lawyer opened the little writing-table, with its yellow satin bag, at which I had often seen the poor old lady writing her notes. He was not long seated there before he abruptly rose, and, turning towards me with an envelope in his hand, said hurriedly,—

'This, no doubt, is what Dorling meant.'

It was directed in my grandmother's writing, which was, however, much more shaky than usual, and the address was,— 'My will. My executors are Mr Bandon, and General Rosemere, C.B.'

'This,' said he, 'is the will of which I know nothing. Very probably it is quite informal. I have here in the bag the will we drew for Lady Duncan, by which you are made her sole heir, as, by every canon of justice, you should be made. But what this contains, or what it is, I have, of course, no idea. I think, for many reasons, I should open it now, and apprise you at once of its contents. But if you prefer waiting until the funeral, I follow your wishes; only this paper may, of course, contain her injunctions as to her funeral.'

I suggested that he should open the envelope at once, and he did so. Lawyers, like doctors, are obliged to learn to mask their faces, and Mr Bandon read to himself the sheet of ordinary white note-paper which he had before him, without comment. When he came to the end, I noticed he examined closely the signatures, and then he shook his head.

No one will ever know what evil spirit took possession of my grandmother's mind on the morning she wrote out herself her new will. As Mr Bandon very clearly explained to me, she had completely disinherited her next-of-kin, who had been brought up by her as her own son, and

who had always tried to do his duty towards her.

'But,' said he, 'cleverly as this is drawn,
and witnessed, she forgot that there is ten
thousand pounds she cannot alienate. If
your father had lived, she could not have
left a shilling away from him, and there
remains this ten thousand pounds in your
father's settlement, which you must have.
But we can see, after the funeral, what
is to be done, and threaten the heir with
a Court of Equity.'

The will, a copy of which lies before me,
and which I would quote, but for the many
legatees mentioned in it, was as clear and
as characteristic as any will could be. I
may, perhaps, be allowed to add that it
was as cruel a will as ever was admitted to
probate. She began with her usual devotion to rank by a bequest of a very fine

Raphael to her neighbour the Duchess
(whose various houses were filled with
European masterpieces).   Her diamond
hoop-ring she bequeathed to another lady
of rank, and a dowager intimate of hers.
Then followed legacies to her two executors, and a long list of her friends in London society, all of whom she remembered
with gifts of money, jewels, or pieces of
plate.   The Dorlings and her coachman
received annuities.   Then, after the ac-
quaintances and the servants, came the
only mention of myself.   'To my grandson, Clare Strong, I leave the sum of five
hundred pounds, and all the plate engraved
with the Strong crest or coat of arms.   I
also leave him all pictures and miniatures,
either in Grosvenor Street or in my house
in Kent, of members of his family, and all
my books.'   The bequest of books was

notable, as, excepting her French library, which consisted of a remarkably risky collection of old French romances, and a certain number of modern novels, she possessed none. The will went on: 'And as to the residue of my property, wheresoever situated, and of whatsoever kind consisting, whether realty or personalty, I give and bequeath the same to my faithful and dear friend, Lord Francis Sherlock, for his own absolute use and benefit.' The signature was written with an effort, but was duly attested by two young Guardsmen.

When I had grasped all this, I felt a change coming over me, and in the few moments of silence which elapsed, I became a different being. I became a man— hard, and cold, and resentful, at all events, for the time. Mr Bandon first spoke.

'As the family lawyer, I decline to act as executor to this will, drawn without my knowledge.'

'And as the heir-at-law, disinherited so cruelly, I decline to remain here another hour. You must communicate with General Rosemere, your co-executor, and I shall at once go to the British Hotel, until I can arrange my plans, and I shall not attend the funeral.'

The lawyer seemed to approve of my resolution.

'I think no one can blame you. That old reprobate, Lord Francis, who is a very rich man, may refuse to benefit by this, but I doubt it. Anyhow, his proposals, if he has any to make, must come through General Rosemere. I will of course, act for you, as always.'

For an instant, to my surprise, I saw a

quiver of his lip, and I knew that he really felt for me. Two hours later, with the Dorlings sobbing farewell at the door, I had left that house for ever.

The body upstairs was upholstered, no doubt, in the old dreary fashion to which we all come, but I never saw her face again—thank God! not even often in my evil dreams.

CHAPTER VI.

LORD FRANCIS SHERLOCK.

'Il est honnête mais médiocre et d'un caractère épi-
neux ; c'est comme la perche, blanche, saine, mais
insipide et pleine d'arêtes.'

IT was clearly my duty, however dreary a
one, to remain in London for the present,
and until my grandmother was buried.
She had left no injunctions as to her
funeral, and I heard afterwards it was
conducted in a decent fashion, and that
she was laid in the same graveyard where
my father lies, in the Bayswater Road.
This is the old cemetery of the Parish of
St George's, Hanover Square, and was
opened after the gronnd at the back of
Mount Street was closed in the year 1764.

There were very few mourners, Lord Francis being the chief one; but Grosvenor Street was blocked with the empty private carriages which followed the hearse. What could be more characteristic of Lady Duncan's life than such a termination?

How I got through those days I never knew. But I had many kind visits from my few real friends, and a great many letters, some of them painful enough. I need scarcely say that, as King David experienced, I also found that 'my kinsmen stood afar off.' They generally do on such occasions, though their overpowering sympathy in the days of one's prosperity is sometimes a little overdone. The day after the funeral, when Mr Bandon was sitting with me in my private room at the hotel, discussing my resources, came a note from General Rosemere.

He began his letter with a few words of
sympathy with me, and deep regret at
Lady Duncan's will; and as Rosemere
was always a gentleman, I believe he
was sincere.   Then he dropped into a
business tone, and said, on behalf of his
co-executor and himself, that they were
most anxious to make everything as little
painful to me as possible.   Lord Francis
had decided to sell both the house in
Grosvenor Street, and also the Kent Cottage.   Of course, everything connected
with my family would be carefully selected,
and sent wherever I directed.   Besides
plate, pictures, and books specified in the
will, anything I had any great fancy for,
Lord Francis wished to be placed at my
disposal; and if I had any liking for the
house in Grosvenor Street, his terms for
the lease would be most friendly ones.

General Rosemere concluded his most polite effusion by hoping we should always remain great friends, and as he was about to be married, he looked forward to presenting me shortly to his wife.

'But the fact remains,' I said, with rather a cynical smile, 'that Lord Francis takes whatever he gets under the will.'

'Precisely so; and, as he is seventy-eight years of age, and a man who has lived every day of his life, he is not likely long to enjoy your fortune. Perhaps he will leave it back to you; but I want to see and to explain to you exactly what your means are. You come of age to-morrow; and I must then give you a written account of my stewardship; but meantime, roughly, the sums are these. Your father left you fifteen thousand pounds in the Funds — all he had in

the world to bequeath. There was ten
thousand pounds in addition, in your
parents' settlement ; but it was not payable
until your grandmother's death. It was,
luckily, settled on the issue of the marriage, so she could not alienate it, and
you now come into it. In addition, Sir
Everard left you three thousand pounds.
We have managed your property as well
as we could, and I think you will find
that, with the ten thousand pounds Con-
sols, you will be worth about twelve hundred pounds a year. A young man can
do very well on that income, even without a profession, if you do not marry, and
you will hardly think of marriage yet.
You have been abominably treated, and
I confess now to you I had hopes Lord
Francis might act as many rich men
would have done under such circum-

stances, and renounced in your favour. But they tell me at the bank he has no intention of doing so, and that your grandmother's bequest to him amounts to at least eighty thousand pounds.'

If you are only twenty-one, and enjoy excellent health, and a present income of twelve hundred pounds a year, life ought to appear to have many possibilities, and to the eye of youth, the absolute independence which now fell to my lot, softened in time the blow the loss of so good a fortune inflicted, and which, to older men, would have seemed irreparable. I received two notes the same evening, both invitations into the country. One was from Lord Francis Sherlock, dated from his country house :—

'SHERLOCK HOUSE.

' DEAR CLARE,—I am an old man, and

you are a young one. Let us accept those relations, and, in spite of what has occurred, most unexpectedly to me, let me be your friend. I was your grandmother's lover; but she would not marry me. *Hinc illæ lacrymæ.* I hate business, and leave it to others, so far as I possibly can. But I told Rosemere to tell you I would do anything you wished, in reason, to oblige you, about the property in the Grosvenor Street house, and also in the country. I can't upset your grandmother's wishes. They must take effect, and I am sorry for it. I am not rich, but still I am too old for legacies; and I am not like that fool Rosemere, who, I hear, is going to marry an Exeter girl without a sixpence. Her father was some pompous, scheming parson there, and her grandfather a farming agent o old Lord Denton. I fear I sha'n't live long enough to see him in his white sheet, and with a flickering halfpenny "dip" in his hand. Fools, and d--d fools, make up the world, and Rosemere comes under the second head. But I run on, and forget the object of my note. Don't be a fool, Clare! Bear no resentment to me ; but come and spend a week at Sherlock next month. I can give you some good shooting later on.—Yours, FRANCIS SHERLOCK.'

The other letter was from Carnaby :—

'DEAREST CLARE,—I have read your letter to Willy, and so know all. I know, too, how brave you will be, and that you will be sure to act, at this important epoch of your life, as your mother—of whom I have so often heard—would have wished. This is your home, and we long for you

to come home. Your room is always filled
with the books and flowers you love best.
We have a few literary people here just
now. Your favourite poet, of the modern
school, is writing a sonnet, and he is so
constantly in the elm avenue, I think it
must be addressed to the rooks. I have
been reading a passage in Southey's
" Doctor," which I have marked for you.
—With Willy's love, your ever affect.,

'MARY PENROSE.'

I have been always, and, even now, as
a middle-aged man, still remain, impulsive
and impetuous when I think I am
wronged, and I really believe I should
now re-write my letter to Lord Francis
Sherlock in nearly the same terms as I
did then. Those terms were these :—

'Mr Clare Strong has to acknowledge

Lord Francis's letter. He considers, under all the circumstances, that Lord Francis, having secured Mr Strong's family fortune, now desires, by addressing such a letter to him, to expressly add insult to the injury he has already inflicted. Mr Clare Strong can only, definitely and finally, state that he does not desire the acquaintance of Lord Francis Sherlock, and that, as regards the will of the late Lady Duncan, he will take what the law gives him, and nothing else. What the law gives him will be arranged between Lord Francis and his professional men of business.'

So there ended any further communication between his lordship and me. I well knew, too, how he would receive such a missive, and could hear, in imagination, the scornful laugh with which he would throw

it into his wastepaper basket.   But, after
all, one of the first luxuries of independence
is to indulge oneself in speaking out one's
mind, as we term it, or, as the Americans
more tersely put it, 'a straight talk.'

Lord Francis Sherlock was a man of
very evil reputation in his county, as
already hinted ; and no ladies ever visited
at his house.   As usual, in such cases, his
misdemeanours were largely exaggerated,
and the air of mystery which he absurdly
affected in his household arrangements,
led to a hundred conjectures, one more
ridiculously untrue than the other.

Sherlock is a very fine place, and was
entailed on the second son of the Duke of
Southam by Lord Francis's grandmother.
For many years it was shut up, but never
let.   Latterly, Lord Francis, in his old
age, had lived there altogether.   Rumour

said truly there was a lady in the house.
Later on, I heard from her lips the whole
story; but, at present, I knew little, except
that the ladies of the county would have
nothing to say with Sherlock, or its master.

I was very tired of London at this
period, and, gladly assenting to my dear
old friend's suggestion to 'come home,'
when I had finished all the business which
the attaining my majority, even in my
small affairs, necessitated, I started off for
Carnaby.

CHAPTER VII.

MRS PENROSE'S GUESTS.

'Telle est la misérable condition des hommes qu'il
leur faut chercher dans la société des consolations aux maux de la Nature et dans la Nature
des consolations aux maux de la société.'

IT was late autumn, and Mrs Penrose had
gathered together an interesting society for
a few days' visit. William had two or three
friends for the cover-shooting, but we all
met at dinner, and, as usual, under the
happy influence of the lady of the manor,
there was much brilliant and amusing
conversation. Mr Eardley, a well-known
writer of those days, and of a very democratic turn of mind, found himself, after

dinner, beside Canon Caryl, whose home
was, at that time, with the Jesuit fathers in
London; and Lady Mary Vivian discussed
literature and politics with both. Mrs
Penrose, moreover, had discovered an extremely interesting man—Mr Auguste de
Chamier—a relation of my own, and a
connoisseur of art, who, without my knowledge hitherto, had lived for years in
Russell Square. He had come to Carnaby with his daughter, a charming girl
of eighteen. It appeared he was a
widower himself, though of an age that
by no means forbade the idea of '*seconde
noce*.' There were also two old maids,
who belonged to that useful genus, common to ordinary English country houses.

Mrs Penrose's dinner table was always
a delightful sight. Fashions change, and,
though her greenhouses and conservatories

were crowded with lovely flowers, they found no place on her round table. But instead, it gleamed with beautiful old silver ornaments and plate of the time of the two Charles' and Queen Anne. The large silver dishes which contained what are now called '*entrées*,' were arranged upon the table on hot-water stands, and from the middle rose a beautiful silver centrepiece, representing both Ceres and Bacchus. I am no judge of these matters, but am told that the thick and bosky woods of modern dinner-tables, and the piled-up masses of rare flowers of new-fashioned ballrooms, are much more effective than the display of family plate. It may be so. And as in these days most family possessions come to the hammer, it is convenient to be able to dispense with them. Still, flowers recklessly thus displayed suggest to my mind an idea of waste, whereas plate remains.

'In a house in which I was once staying,' Mr Eardley was remarking, 'there is a most marvellous display of plate in the private chapel. This plate was church loot in one of the great wars, and came mostly from Spain. It remained at the bank in London for many years, only produced at great dinner parties in the London house. The owner of it all died, and, being childless, his nephew succeeded him. The nephew was a man of strong religious views, and of Catholic bias, though he never was received into the Roman Church. His first act, on succeeding to the property, was to re-dedicate this plate, and there it stood on the altar in his own chapel, on all holy days. He is dead now, and his son is selling it all, to pay his gambling debts.

What an opportunity for some of your rich friends, Caron Caryl! for there is no doubt it all came from Catholic churches in Spain and Portugal.'

'You are quite right; and I may re-assure you,' said the Canon, with a bright smile, 'for it is to be bought in. Still, you will agree with me, to retain cathedral plate, stolen from the professors of one faith, and to apply it to the uses of an-other and totally opposed religion, was not a very logical act. To restore it, I grant you, would have been grand. To utilise it as it was utilised, was illogical; and to sell it, I am afraid, is mean.'

'Which shows that meanness leads to a good result—the restoration of stolen goods,' laughed Lady Mary Vivian.

'It is a remarkable year for sales,' went on Eardley. 'In the present unsettled

state of Europe, with revolutions apparently imminent in almost every country,
and with Chartists here, the great families, and even the European Courts, are
awaking to a sense of danger and inse-
curity. I hear the great Vere collection
of jewels is to be sold privately. Men feel
they must realise the value of their possessions, and especially of their diamonds,
before they cease to be valued in the
democratic Arcadia, to which we shall
all come.'

'You will see, as has happened before,'
said Mrs Penrose, 'things will settle
down once more, and this year be only
recollected as an interesting epoch. As
for diamonds, the ladies of the Great Revolution admired and collected them as
eagerly as those of the *ancien régime.*'

'The late Marquis de Tourville, your

great-great uncle, Mr Strong,' remarked
M. de Chamier, 'was guillotined for his
loyalty to his master, and his large property in Picardy was confiscated. It
was known he had ancestral diamonds
of enormous value ; but they disappeared.
Since I have lived in London, I have had
opportunities of tracing these jewels. The
Marquis sold them in 1787, and they are
now in various famous collections here of
your ancient families. He did what Mr
Eardley says others are doing at this very
moment.'

At that instant, the dining-room windows
being opened, owing to the unusual heat of
the autumn evening, a sound attracted the
attention of us all, though to some of us
it was familiar enough. The church bell
was tolling monotonously.

'Ah, you wonder what service, Canon,

can be proceeding at this hour, on a Tuesday evening. In this year of revolutions, you are listening to the Curfew Bell. It has been rung here for many, many generations, and, as some antiquarians believe, from the date of the church's first erection. There is a bequest to the ringer, which is lost, like the creation of the first peerage of Mar, in antiquity. But at all events, it has been rung here for several hundred years: that is proved by the parish books. However, we do not "cover the embers, or put out the light," but leave you gentlemen to your wine; and when you feel inclined to join us in the saloon, we will have some music.'

And the ladies left the room.

'Carnaby,' observed Mr Eardley, as we all settled round a horseshoe table near

a small fire, 'is the most feudal parish I
know in England.'

William Penrose, at one end of the
table, was deeply engrossed in a *tête-à-tête*
conversation with a friend as to their day's
sport. So Eardley's sermon was not addressed to that end of the table.

'As a Radical, I think the old system
wrong. The family living; and the model
village—in which not even a public-house
is allowed—the absolute dependence of
every single human item in this place,
including the parson, on Mrs Penrose's
simple dictum, is, to my mind, degrading
in theory.

> " God bless the Squire, and his relations,
>   And keep us all in our proper stations ! "

But when I come to actual facts here,
I find, owing to the exalted character of
our hostess, and her absolute sense of

duty and unselfishness, that everything has
worked excellently well, and that, though
the Curfew Bell tolls nightly over Carnaby,
there is no village in England better cared
for, and no landlord who has done his
duty more nobly than Mrs Penrose. She
has restored her church, and increased its
endowment. She has made her village an
artistic treat. As I walked down it this
afternoon, every cottage was a picture,
and its inmates the perfection of clean-
liness, health, and contentment. She has
built the schools here, and herself constantly superintends them. When you
speak of her to her tenants, you can see
they adore her, and at the thought of her
sorrows in the past, their eyes fill with
tears. No! the theory is a degrading
one; but, in the hands of a noble and intellectual man or woman, it can, no doubt,

be made to work far better than a good
system in bad hands.   But the noble and
intellectual are the minority in this world
—the small minority, and always will
be.'

We all listened to this exordium, as
interesting from a pronounced Radical
doctrinaire, who was very fond of an
audience ; but the sound of music came
floating into the room, and one by one we
rose, attracted to the saloon.   Mademoiselle
de Chamier, who had a fine contralto voice,
was singing an English song, privately
printed, called ' The Shadows on the Wall.'
Her voice, without being of the highest
order, was a sweet and pathetic one ; and
I confess to preferring simple and pathetic
songs, sung with expression, to those
elaborate *tours de force*, which, no doubt,
are marvels, as the work of a human

organ, but leave one unmoved, and un-
sympathetic.

After which confession, it must remain
on record that I am not a musician.
Canon Caryl's career had been a chequered
one, and originally he served in the Royal
Navy. With a little persuasion, he sent
for his guitar, and, accompanying himself,
sang that delightful naval ballad 'Sweet
Alice Benbolt.' As the final lines were
given, in a wonderfully melodious, though
not powerful, voice,—

'They fitted a grey marble slab to a tomb,
And fair Alice lies under the stone,'

I confess I walked to the window, and
gazed at the red harvest moon, sailing
across the sky, above the solemn avenue
of elms. After the usual jovial hour and
a half in the gunroom, with William for

the most cheery of hosts, we went to bed, and I found myself suddenly thinking, with all the *insouciance* of twenty-one, that I had scarcely addressed a single word the whole evening to my newly - found cousin,—a charming girl, whose Christian name I did not even know, and resolving to atone for the neglect, I fell asleep.

CHAPTER VIII.

IDA DE CHAMIER.

'Beyond the reach of time or fate,
   These graces shall endure,
Still, like the passion they create,
   Eternal, constant, pure.'

PEOPLE talk of the 'mist of years,' and no
doubt, in retrospect, much we have done,
and seen, and thought, appears in a haze;
yet, thereout stand simple and apparently
unimportant incidents which have affected
our entire life, and which once more evoke
the often asked question, 'Are we the sport
of a defined, uncontrollable destiny, an
inexorable Kismet, to which it is best to
bow, or is there indeed—

"A Providence which shapes our ends,
Rough-hew them as we may"?'

The morning found me strolling, after
breakfast, through the park at Carnaby,
with my cousin, M. de Chamier.   It was
a brilliant autumn day, and the sun lighted
up the fine trees, and the distant view,
which, though not a grand one from any
part of the domain, is exquisitely English,
and pastoral.

'I never saw your grandmother,' he was
saying, 'although my near relative,—in
fact, my first cousin.   My father was her
father's brother ; but he did not marry
until quite late in life, which accounts for
the difference in Lady Duncan's and my
age.   I once wrote to her, reminding her
of my existence, and our near relationship ;
but she never replied.   The truth was,
she judged my motives according to the

standard of the wretched world she lived in, and she could not understand that my only reason for writing was a family feeling, which in us Huguenots has always been strong. It is very singular how devoid she was of it, and I daresay she would have been amazed to have learned that nothing would have induced me to allow my daughter Ida to know her friends, or to have mixed among them.'

I told him the details of her will, with all of which he was not acquainted; and in expressing his horror, he asked what had become of her diamonds.

'The Chamier diamonds were famous, and your grandmother had a considerable share of them. Some were sold, as I think I told you last night, at the time of the great Revolution, or rather, I should say, just before it, but others were taken by my uncle to Geneva, and deposited for safety in the bank there, and afterwards bequeathed to your grandmother.'

'Oh, yes,' I replied, 'she often wore them,—in fact, a few days before her death. They have gone to Lord Francis Sherlock, and are no doubt now decorating the lady who graces Sherlock, as I hear, with her presence.'

Of course I spoke with bitterness, and my cousin did not remonstrate, but changed the subject.

'You must come and see us when we return to London. I have been collecting prints all my life. You will be interested in those of your French ancestors, of which I have a large number. My daughter is a great companion for me, and she takes an interest in all my tasks. I am glad I have no other child. She is enough for me.

'But our branch dies out then in the male line?'

'The English branch dies out, if I have no son, at my death; but the French elder branch is very numerous.'

We were strolling back once more, and had reached the wide extent of flower beds which cover the terraces at Carnaby, when we met Canon Caryl, returning from some antiquarian researches in the church, with Mademoiselle de Chamier.

'Ida delights in old monuments and family histories,' said her father to me, as she approached.

She was an extremely pretty girl, with a suspicion of French extraction, not without its charm. She had the dark hair and large limpid brown eyes which my grandmother must have had in her youth, a fine clear, healthy skin, a small nose, and a very mobile, clever mouth. But she was small in figure, although remarkably well made, and inclined to be stout. She carried herself extremely well, and had—what used to be considered an attraction—a very short waist. But her manner was charming—all vivacity and intelligence, characterised by a great desire to please, and a total absence of all *gêne.* She presented a strange contrast to the tall slender figure, bowed slightly with age, of her companion, Canon Caryl, whose eagle eye, and aquiline nose, and courtly manner, betokened intellect, descent, and mental struggle. He broke into one of his somewhat superficial smiles.

'We have been indulging in a little ancient history, Monsieur de Chamier, and your daughter is so good as not to be bored.'

Certainly, she did not look bored.

'Oh, papa! it is one of the most interesting old churches I have ever seen. There is a monument there of Sir Willoughby Denton, and his wife, who lived in the reign of Charles I., which is perfectly lovely; and such a curious story about it, the Canon has been telling me.'

'And what is the story?' I ventured to ask.

'Nothing very remarkable,' observed Canon Caryl, as the young lady turned from me to him for an explanation. 'Sir Willoughby did not belong to this county. He hailed from Staffordshire, and was of a devout family of the Church, and also a staunch Royalist in later years. He came here, however, and married one of Mrs Penrose's ancestresses. He lies under the chancel. History tells that Dorothy, Lady Denton, died at the birth of her first child. Sir Willoughby was broken-hearted at her death, and her child died also. The monument to which Mademoiselle de Chamier alludes, is one of the most perfect of its time, in England. There are three effigies—Sir Willoughby, and his wife, and the baby, the latter swathed, after the manner of Italian children. The sad record remains that Sir Willoughby married again, and is buried with his second wife in Staffordshire, so that this beautiful effigy of him here has rather a cynical effect on the county historian, who knows his subsequent story.'

'Well,' said M. de Chamier, 'it is only the usual melancholy moral, which I won't repeat before two young people; but Sir Willoughby ought to have had his effigy removed to the grave he elected to lie in.'

Mr Eardley had joined us, and remarked,—' Did you ever see the fresco in

Leicestershire of the Day of Judgment, where the two wives are depicted, amid an array of bones all flying into their proper places, in a state of bewilderment before the skeleton of a second husband, like your Sir Willoughby?'

Canon Caryl, observing drily, 'That difficulty was answered more than eighteen hundred years ago,' turned away.

M. de Chamier, whose religious views were not quite so precise and defined as those of his Huguenot ancestors, joined Mr Eardley in some religious argument, and I took the opportunity of turning with my fair cousin into one of the wooded paths which at Carnaby lead to innumerable summer-houses, fish-ponds, and the famous bowling-green.

'How very odd,' I said, with all the frankness of youth, 'that you and I, Ida,

should not have met before. I may call
you Ida, as we are such near relations,
may I not?'

It will thus be seen that I was not, even
at that age, shy. It would have been impossible for anyone brought up as I was
to have been bashful in the presence even
of so divine a creature, as further inspection led me mentally to conclude Ida de
Chamier to be.

'Of course we are nearly first cousins;
and I have so few English relations, that
it is delightful to have found a new
one.'

'Exactly what I feel. All my friends
have so many cousins, and uncles, and
aunts, and I seem to have none. So let
us, I hope, if you will, be great friends.'

Though several years my junior, she
answered (as girls are generally more ad-

vanced in their ideas than boys of the same age), with some demureness,—

'I hope, and so does papa, that you will come and see us in London.'

'Of course I shall; but I am not quite decided yet whether I shall spend the winter in London. In fact, I am not decided about anything. You see my position has been so altered this year, that I sometimes feel I ought to work, and earn money, if I could do so. I might get called to the Bar, for instance. But what I always have in my mind is the wish to travel. I *long* to travel.'

'And who so independent and free to do so as yourself?' said Mademoiselle de Chamier. 'I always wish I had been born a man. My life is passed in a very narrow groove; but then I always feel I am everything to my father; and we have travelled together in Europe a good deal. But politics are so disturbed just now that no English are abroad, I suppose.'

'Then you winter in London this year?'

'Either in London or at Brighton. My father is fond of Brighton. He is not now in business, but still he likes to go to the city sometimes, and so to be within reach of London. He is very clever, and a great reader. I daresay you have found that out already.'

I am afraid my interest in my fair cousin had rather absorbed any curiosity I might have felt as to my newly-discovered relative's abilities. It seemed to me that he was rather selfish in so totally appropriating his delightful daughter's charms and talents to himself, as he appeared to have done. I forgot that Ida was only eighteen

years of age, as she spoke with the force
and gravity which an only and motherless
girl often acquires.

We had reached the bowling-green,
and sat down under the shade of the
old elms. Suddenly she said,—

'I always think a place like this
does one good. It makes one realise the
vulgarity of the riotous world without.
Here is rest, tranquillity, content. Two
hundred years ago, it was as it is to-day.
No striving, no emulation, no disappointment, and no disturbing tragedy or passion ; and then the churchyard close by.'

A sweet voice, very familiar to me,
suddenly interrupted,—

' My dear child, you are too young to
talk about churchyards. Leave such
thoughts to old women like me!' Mrs
Penrose had interrupted our *tête-à-tête*,

and, dearly as I loved her, I could not, for a moment, forgive her. But she went on lightly, 'I want to know if you two young people care to drive with me this afternoon. Perhaps, Clare, you would drive us, and take charge of the cobs. There is a beautiful old manor house about eight miles from here, un-inhabited, but in perfect order, which, oddly enough, Clare, belongs to Lord Francis Sherlock. He keeps it up exactly as it was, and it really was the original house of his mother's family, before they grew rich, and inherited Sherlock, in William the Third's reign. Your father tells me, Mademoiselle de Chamier, you take an interest in antiquities, and might perhaps like to see this curious house. I don't know, Clare, if the fact that it belongs to Lord Francis will render the visit disagreeable; but, of course, do exactly as you like.'

I hastened to say—I am afraid a little impatiently, for I still wanted to continue my conversation with Ida—that I should be delighted to drive the ladies over, and that the fact of the owner being Lord Francis Sherlock was a matter of perfect indifference to me, as there was no possibility of meeting him there. The carriage which came to the door after luncheon, was an old-fashioned waggonette, and as Mrs Penrose took a footman with her, to my chagrin I found myself debarred from any further conversation with my cousin, who sat with Mrs Penrose, her father, and Canon Caryl. Mr Eardley and Lady Mary did not join the party. The footman, I was obliged mentally to admit, at my side, was an unpleasant necessity, as

I did not know the route ; and the cobs,
a recent purchase, being very fresh, soon,
of necessity, engrossed all my thoughts.
It struck me afterwards, as a coincidence,
that I should thus find myself driving to
view one of the possessions of a man who
had so cruelly defrauded me of my inheritance, and who had been an admirer
and a suitor of my grandmother's.   We at
length arrived at a very humble swinging
gate, without any lodge, and, driving in,
passed through several grass fields, and
two or three other gates.   Suddenly the
road took a sharp turn, and, under a
short and perfectly straight avenue of
lime trees, we pulled up before one of
the most beautiful old houses I have ever
seen in this or any other country.   A
most elaborate old iron-work gate fronted
the house, which was of red brick, with

a large façade, and two small wings.
There was a grass courtyard, and a narrow path, up which we all walked to the
simple doorway, over which was the
Sherlock shield, with the motto, '*Nil nisi
Deo.*' The centre part of the building was
manifestly much older than the wings,
which had been added in the reigns of
the two Charles'. As we entered the
quaint hall, with its magnificent carved
oak ceiling, Mrs Penrose explained to
the caretaker of the house, who respect-
fully saluted her, 'I want to show the
house myself.' 'All this part of the
house,' she added to us, 'belongs to the
time of Henry the Seventh. It has not
been altered in any single respect, so far
as one can see, since it was built. Of
course, the furniture here, as you perceive,
is mostly of Queen Anne's time; and

there is a delightful cradle upstairs in
one of the bedrooms, also of that date,
and made of solid oak.' Mademoiselle
de Chamier was delighted, as also the
Canon, with all they saw. The staircase,
with its shallow stairs, and carved designs
and legends, especially interested the
Canon, as also the old chapel, a most
diminutive and rather bare room.

I, too, was charmed with this present
and living picture of a home of one's ancestors three hundred years ago, showing
exactly how men of gentle birth and
moderate fortune lived in those far-a-way
times ; but I confess to the weakness of
human nature in muttering to myself,
'To think *this*, too, should belong to
that graceless old reprobate, who probably does not care a straw for all these
wonderful antiquities.' But I was wrong.

Lord Francis Sherlock, like many of his kind, had many sides to his character, and at one time of his life had devoted much time and money to the place; and I recollected afterwards that my grandmother had once long ago spoken to me of this house, and of his interest in it.

'The manor has only a small property attached to it,' said Mrs Penrose, 'and, I believe, only a couple of farms. Moreover, it is unentailed, so Lord Francis can leave it as he chooses. Sherlock is entailed on his elder brother's second son, but the manor of Elcote has not been entailed for a century.'

Through the various bedrooms, with their quaint beds, and looking-glasses, and latticed windows, to the powder closet, where the ladies of the household resorted

for hair powdering, to the museum, where
Lord Francis, in glass cases, had stored
many curious documents, coins, medals,
and old prints, we all wandered in delightful gossip, Ida asking constant questions,
and Mrs Penrose decking everything with
romance and sentiment.   We came down
another staircase, and small, comparatively,
as the house was, it seemed easy enough
to lose one's way.   A large bush of
mistletoe hung suspended in the hall,
to which we had again returned, and
which Mrs Penrose told us was only
renewed from Christmas to Christmas.
It looked a little brown and withered,
and Ida took no notice of it, and I
dared not make any facetious remark
about it.

'And now, Mrs Penrose,' said Ida, 'for
the ghost.   It is impossible for such a

house as this to exist and for no ghostly
tradition to belong to it. Let us sit down
here on these remarkably uncomfortable
high-backed chairs, and hear the ghost
story.'

'There is, I believe, a ghost story
belonging to the house; but I don't believe in ghosts, and it is better to
forget such stories. So far, however, I may tell you that it is connected with a tradition that whoever
inherits this manor, either never marries, or, if he marries, does so at his
peril.'

'Is that founded on a religious oath?'
asked Canon Caryl.

'No,' replied Mrs Penrose,—'on some
old story of a wrong and a curse. But
let us come into the garden, and see the
other side of the house.'

Some beautiful turf of considerable extent lay beyond the glass door, opening into the so-called garden, which in reality was only laid out in grass. On one side of the house was quite a vast orchard, and I endeavoured to attract Ida to visit this with me, under an assumed interest in the apple harvest; but she seemed to avoid another *tête-à-tête*. The sun had been shining brightly, but suddenly became obscured. Everything to me looked grey and chill, even the house we had just quitted. Our hostess seemed to feel the general depression, and predicted a storm. So once more we entered the carriage, and, not well pleased, I drove the cobs home at a needlessly hurried pace. The depression was clearly explained by a roll of thunder, and heavy drops of rain, as we rattled up the solemn avenue at Carnaby.

At dinner, that night, our conversation naturally turned much upon Elcote. Mr Eardley, as usual, was the chief spokesman.

' Delightful, no doubt, theoretically ! Picturesque exterior, and charming specimen of early Tudor domestic architecture. But what about living in such a house the present day? Did you notice if the floors slanted in an unpleasant way ? Were there fire-places in all the bedrooms, and how about the ventilation ? Bells, of course, there were none, and drains were best unmentioned. Oh, no, the sentiment is charming, but I prefer a house like this, which has been modernised internally, and which has kept pace with the times. I like comfort, and comfort means progress.

It is all very well for Lord Francis Sherlock to keep Elcote up, as you say he
does, but he takes very good care to live
himself at Sherlock, where nothing, I will
be bound, is sacrificed to antiquarian interest which could conduce to the comfort
of its possessor.'

'Ah! Mr Eardley, you pose as a
democrat and a cynic, and I never will
believe you are either,' murmured Mrs
Penrose.

' I could not be a cynic,' he said,
with a little bow; 'at least in this
house.'

We had no music that evening, but
were very merry over a round game of
cards, and never noticed the Curfew Bell.
Not once again had I an opportunity to
speak alone with my cousin. The fates
seemed against me. When she said 'Good-

night,' she raised her lovely brown eyes most unconsciously to mine, though I ventured on the slightest pressure of her fingers, and said, in her most bewitching half French manner,—

'Take care you do not dream of the Elcote ghost. I am sure there *is* a ghost.'

That evening, in the dear old smoking-room, where William and I had passed so many pleasant evenings, recalling the jokes and good stories of our school and college days, we once more found ourselves alone, our elders having retired to bed. One of William's invariable customs was, when the men came to the smoking-room, before he joined them, to go up to his mother's room, where he generally remained for at least a quarter of an hour. They were so wrapped up in each other,

that, before sleep, this nightly interview
alone was a sacred habit.   She had no
one now but him to confide in, to clasp
to her heart, and even I, though so intimate a friend of his, never knew what
passed between them on these occasions.
But, to-night, William, when he joined me,
seemed rather more serious than usual,
and, after we had lighted our pipes and
filled our glasses, he said, without hesita-
tion,—

'I am glad those "grave and potent
seniors" have deserted us to-night.   I want
to make some plans with you.   I have
decided to give up the hunting, after all,
this winter, if you will go with me to
America ; and I think we might have a
very pleasant time of it.   Mother gives
me three months of absence.   She says
she can't spare either you or me longer.

But we could do a good deal in that time. What do you say?'

'Agreed!' I exclaimed joyfully, forgetting everything else; 'if you really think you would like it.'

'You see,' he said, 'for one thing, your plans are so unsettled; and you have no home but this at present; and I don't think you had better settle down in chambers just yet. So this winter seems an opportunity for the travel which we have so often talked about; and I shall have many a hunting season here after this year; so let us go!'

It was not then that I realised how unselfish he was in this proposal; and not till long afterwards, that it was my second mother who had suggested the self-denying act he was too ready to perform. His was a noble nature; and life, alas! has taught me how few there are like him, in the desire to make others happy at whatever self-sacrifice.   When we said goodnight, the plan of a journey to the States was settled.

CHAPTER IX.

OUR VOYAGE.

'The lawyer and the usurer,
  That sit in gowns of fur,
  In closets warm can take no harm,
  Abroad they need not stir.
  When winter fierce with cold doth pierce,
  And beats with hail and snow,
  We are sure to endure,
  When the stormy winds do blow.'

My life had hitherto been almost exclu-
sively spent on *terra firma*, and my marine
journeys had been short and infrequent.
Consequently, when William and I found
ourselves on board a vessel, needless to
say, very different to the magnificent
steamers which now cross the Atlantic,
and which are more luxurious than most

hotels, it was a great moment of excitement for me. Our steamer was one of the largest, most comfortable, and the quickest, of those days; but the journey was seldom then accomplished from Liverpool to New York under a fortnight, and often occupied a much longer time. We had the first officer's cabin to ourselves, and were, in every respect, most comfortable. I remember waking up the first day out, early in the morning, and looking out of our porthole. So far as eye could reach, of course, was dull, monotonous ocean; and, as it happened, not even a sail in sight. The thought occurred to me, then, and often has done so since, what an apparent uselessness there is in such a vast expanse of water, and, for what purpose, if any, could it have been created. But the sea has always been suggestive to me of many things, and a death which occurred shortly afterwards on board, gave me weird and strange dreams. It was late at night, in a perfectly calm sea, except for that sweep of wave which is always present in the Atlantic, and with a brilliant moon riding overhead, that the coffin was lowered into the beautiful ocean,—' Until the sea gives up her dead.' She is very tenacious of them now, and the moan of the waves, and wind, which was rising, was not suggestive of any resurrection. The next day, there was a storm. All night I had been kept awake by the roar of the wind, the creaking and straining, and the horrible sensation when a big sea has been taken on board,— the cessation of the sound of the machinery, and that awful tremble which seems to invest a ship with humanity, struggling against the elements. I was not sea-sick, as my poor friend was; but the sea was so tremendous, and the rolling and pitching so fearful, that it was impossible, for two days, to get on deck. When I was able to do so, I saw a grand sight, familiar no doubt to thousands, but new to me at that date. A sailor gave me his arm as I mounted the companion, and I beheld what landsmen mean, when they talk of the sea being 'mountains high.' Our gallant steamer looked as if she would be overwhelmed, as the huge waves environed her, and she plunged into the trough of the ocean. The sky wore a wild appearance. Scudding clouds flew across the horizon, and all around were the ravages of the gale, which now had spent its fury. I remember thinking how little the small interests of one's life seemed in such a grand scene as this. My poor old grandmother,

and her wicked will, my bitterness towards Lord Francis Sherlock, my passion
(as I termed it) for Ida de Chamier, the
hurricane seemed to blow all these things
away. And I thought of the grand words
of King David,—

> 'These see the works of the Lord, and His
> wonders in the deep. For He commandeth
> and raiseth the stormy wind which lifteth up
> the waves thereof. They mount up to the
> heaven, they go down again to the depths,'
> etc.

The truth is, that it does a man good, at
any age, to face God and Nature, and to
forget, for a time, the petty chicaneries
which must always surround even a
noble life, and, much more so an ordinary one. After that day, we had no
more rough weather. William recovered
his spirits, and his head, and came also
on deck. How lovely the nights were!
I have crossed the Atlantic, and also

the Pacific Ocean, several times since, but
I have never again seen such wonderful
effects in the sky at night. The heavens
seemed ablaze with shooting stars—the
fireworks of the Celestials. The sea
at night was brilliantly luminous with
phosphorus, which lighted up the beautiful
rollers, churned into many colours by our
screw. To me was new then that lovely
ultra-marine tint of waves, which one never
sees except in mid-ocean.

Our fellow-passengers were not interesting to us, as they mostly seemed men of
business; and the ladies were few, and
very different in appearance and class to
the fascinating persons who crowd the
decks of the modern Cunarder in the
summer-time, and who look upon a trip
to the 'other side' as little more than an
excursion from Portsmouth to the Isle of

Wight. We did not escape fog altogether in the neighbourhood of Newfoundland: I think very few voyagers across the Atlantic ever do.

A fog at sea is absolutely dangerous and uncomfortable, and has no elements of grandeur or interest. It is, besides, far more perilous than heavy weather. But in those days competition was so much less that we slackened speed very considerably, and did not rush on, as I understand many modern companies insist upon their captains doing, prepared to assert that such speed in a fog constitutes no special danger.

We were very glad, however, to see the sun again, and to anchor, after a rather tedious voyage, outside the bar at Sandy Hook.

As everyone has been to America, it

might be advisable not to give, even cursorily, my unimportant impressions of the country; but I will go so far as to say that there was nothing I saw in my travels there which struck me so much as the harbour of New York. My views are often morbid, and I should like to rest, when I die, in the Greenwood Cemetery, overlooking the finest scene in the world. It is finer now than it was then, as the extent of shipping is so vastly increased. But to my dying day I shall remember that bright November morning when we steamed leisurely past the forts, and for the first time I saw the great unbeautiful commercial city beneath a blue sky, and without a suggestion of smoke, and with the most romantic surroundings in the clear distant air.

The last time I entered New York harbour my feelings were different. I was a middle-aged, disappointed man, and some of my disappointment was connected with the great country I now visited for the last time. Coney Island, with its monster elephant, seemed the acme of vulgarity. I only saw the exaggeration of Brooklyn Bridge; and the green hills far away were inferior to the Cotswolds. Jersey City was simply hideous; and the various dockyards of the steam companies the incarnation of ugliness. How blessed is youth!

Slowly we made our progress, and I longed to leap on shore, full of enthusiasm for the new scenes, the new manners, the new food, and the new friends. There were the usual tiresome delays about landing, which, perforce, restrained my impetuosity, and called forth much violent

language on the part of William, who
explained that the moment you arrived
in a country which boasted of free institutions, it was absolutely necessary to
be emphatic in the expression of indi-
vidual opinion.

But at last we were rattled along through
very mean streets and over the most un-
easy paving stones, to our hotel in the
neighbourhood of Washington Square.
Such a vast city has now spread west-
ward towards Central Park, that this
situation, I presume, would not now be
fashionable ; but at this time it was sufficiently central, and afforded us every
possible comfort, and even luxury, according to the report given by the servant who had accompanied us.

I afterwards found that taking a servant
to America was the greatest possible mis-

take, as it gave an altogether exaggerated idea of our wealth, which led to proportionate fleecing.

The hospitality of Americans cannot, now or then, be too highly eulogised; and with the letters of introduction we carried, hotels were not likely to be long a necessity. New York was still empty. After a wet summer had come one of those lovely Indian autumns for which the country is proverbial, and consequently the great people of New York had not yet returned to the city. The heat, indeed, was most unusual for the time of year, and we were both well pleased, having done the ordinary sightseeing, to step on board a well-equipped private steamer, which conveyed us up the Hudson, in the course of about five hours, to the residence of Mr Buer, a rich

merchant, who had given us a cordial welcome to his country place.

I do not think any one ever forgets his
first impressions of the autumn foliage of
America, and as we steamed along we
were both mute with delight at the marvellous colouring which both banks of the
grand river displayed. In some cases, the
maples, with their brilliant yellow leaves,
had scarlet trunks, which effect for a time
we did not perceive was due to the Virginia
creeper which clung round them. There
is a wonderful stillness, too, in the American atmosphere at this time of year, which
gives an indescribable effect to this mass
of colour. There is death in the air, but
Nature dies in the hey-day of her beauty,
and with the dignity of Hecuba, as described by Euripides.

Our landing-stage reached, our host was

there in his phaeton to receive us. He was not at all effusive in his manner at first, rather a silent, middle-aged man, with scarcely any accent, but full of intelligence and culture. In short, he was exactly the reverse of every American I have ever seen presented on the stage or in current literature. One passion I at once discovered in him during our drive, namely, for horses, of which, it appeared, he bred a great many for his own amusement and also profit. The two are seldom apart in America. For politics he cared nothing at all, although he foresaw the revolution which was bound to come, and spoke to me once or twice of the effects the inevitable victory of the North would have on the country generally. His horses flew along at a marvellous pace, and, not being quite free from the American love of dis-

play, as we were careering on a straight
bit of road, at a pace which caused the
loose stones to fly up in my face as I held
firmly on, he suddenly threw the reins
down, and the horses came to a dead stop.
It was a piece of theatrical effect which
caused William to again indulge in an
expletive, but *sotto voce* on this occasion.

Mr Buer's park was not at all what we
understand by the term. We turned suddenly off the road, through a plantation of
maples, tulip trees, and the American oak,
and soon drove up in front of a handsome
modern house—according to English ideas,
an extremely handsome villa. Below the
house was an artificial lake with two or
three islands. There were no flower-beds,
but the beautifully-coloured trees supplied
their place, and there was plenty of turf.
A verandah ran round the entire house,

and the view, with distant mountains, was extremely fine. Still, as William observed to me later, ' it did not look quite finished.' Mr Buer was a bachelor, and we were quite unprepared for the bevy of young ladies who appeared in the drawing-room before dinner. Our host had told us not to dress for dinner, so, of course, we obeyed his orders, and imagined we were to discuss a very simple bachelor repast. It was rather embarrassing to us both to find an elderly lady, who was introduced as Miss Buer, our host's sister, no less than four young ladies, and a young gentleman, whose accent was far from being so subdued as that of our host. The ladies were all exquisitely dressed and bejewelled. Be it distinctly understood they were ladies in dress, manner, and cultivation of mind, and it ought not to be necessary to say so, were it not that one hears so many strange stories of *Américaines* in Europe, who do not come up to this standard. But the explanation is, that we see the worst side of their society, and I have no doubt the evil will increase until society in Paris and London will receive the *demi monde* of the States.

Miss Buer acted the useful part of Greek Chorus in the establishment. She explained us all to each other, and was a most useful accessory to the whole party for our host, as already said, seemed at first a silent man.

I never ate a better dinner. It was cooked, Miss Buer informed us, by a man of colour, and a first-rate cook he seemed to be. The attendants, too, were all niggers. When I next visited New York, I might have been in Grafton Street, and there was not a black man in service; and one need not go to America to decide on the merits of Irish cookery.

The four young ladies were all cousins of one another, and all nieces of the Buers. The one I took in to dinner was remarkably handsome—Miss Angelina Pike. She had the finest bust and shoulders for so young a girl (she could not be more than nineteen) that I have ever seen.

'How did I like New York?'

'Well,' I said, 'of course, it's a very fine city, but one seems rather out of place as an idler. Everyone seems bent on dollars. But if you ask me about the harbour, you'll find me an enthusiast.'

'You come along to Baltimore. I'm going back there on Saturday. I'm a Baltimore girl; and my ma means to ask you two gentlemen to stay with us. My cousin Ella, who went in with your friend to dinner, lives in Baltimore, too, and my other two cousins live in New York.'

'Mary Buer is my brother John's daughter, and lives in Fifth Avenue,' said the Greek Chorus ; 'and so does Susan ; but Angelina and Ella Pike, my two sisters' children, live at Baltimore.'

It appeared to me that William was having a very lively flirtation with Miss Ella Pike, a small but pretty blonde with a gay manner ; and it seemed a fortunate coincidence that both these cousins, being so handsome and agreeable, lived at Baltimore, whither we also were bound. In deference to English customs, the negroes constantly passed the champagne, and Mr Buer kept us company, though he professed not to drink wine.

'When you get to Baltimore, sir, mind

you ask my brother-in-law, Pike, for some
of his rain-water Madeira ; but he is sure
to give you some whether you ask for it or
not. Terrapin, and old Baltimore Madeira,
is no bad providing.'

After dinner, the weather was so mild,
that we all adjourned to the verandah,
from which a glorious sunset, or rather
the remains of it, in gold and crimson
clouds, charmed one's eye. We sipped
our coffee, and presently the two Miss
Pikes and the two Miss Buers came down
with their banjoes, and gave us delicious
music. First, the two Miss Pikes sang
comic negro songs : one about the ark was
a trifle profane ; but, as Buer himself admitted, 'real witty.' Then they broke into
the pathetic Virginian air, familiar to
Europeans, with its beautifully melodious
chorus. These young ladies were so

amiable, and so delighted to give us the pleasure which they saw on all our faces, that it was quite dark as they all four sang a lovely quartette, called 'The old Kentucky Shore.' As we moved into the house, Buer said, 'Do you hear the Katydids?'

'Katydid, Katydid, Katydid.'

It was the monotonous cry of the bird which sings continuously in American woods when the summer is over, and seemed to me a melancholy sound. But I soon forgot it, as we adjourned to a most luxurous smoking-room, where our host did the honours in the most hospitable style, and where he insisted on brewing himself for me one of those elaborate American 'drinks,' of which I confess no appreciation, except so far as the ice is concerned. Mr Buer was in advance of his

time, for he told us he often went over
to Europe.

'My business is chrome,' he said, 'and
my father made a big pile in it ; but we
Americans are never content until we
make a big pile bigger, so we brothers are
pretty busy men, and I go over to the
other side on business. I'm a richer man
than my brothers, but that's only because
I am a bachelor. We don't have big
families in America, as you do in England ;
but still it stands to reason a single man
is richer than a married man. You must
see my house in New York. I have some
fine pictures there, mostly French ones.'

If Mr Buer now talked a good deal
about himself and his belongings, as he
undoubtedly did, neither William nor I
found his conversation dull. He was full
of information, and all he told us about

himself, had the great merit to us of novelty.

'To-morrow morning you'll come along and look at my stables, which may, perhaps, rather surprise you. But Englishmen don't, as a rule, care for our horses. We shall see what you say. You ought to ride well, sir,' he added, turning to William.

It was an instance of American intuition; for William was one of the best horsemen I ever knew, and one of the hardest riders in the Midlands.

'Yes; perhaps; I'm pretty well at home outside a horse; but how did you guess that?'

'Can't say, sir; but you look like a man who can ride.'

I found, to my surprise, that Buer was extremely well read in eighteenth century English literature, and seemed to know his Shakespeare almost by heart. His library contained all the standard authors of the eighteenth century, and some of his books were curious and scarce editions. He told me Pope was his favourite poet, which seemed a strange taste for an American. When I suggested that Bolingbroke wrote some of Pope's couplets, he said shortly,—

'And Bacon, I suppose, the best of Shakespeare's plays?'

'No,' I said, 'I despise the Englishman who believes that.'

'And so do I, as an American. When I went to England first, I went to Stratford; but it seemed to me you English don't revere that great man's memory as we should do.'

'Or, we revere it in a different way.'

He did not reply, as wishing to avoid disputatious matter.

'Well, gentlemen, I sit up late, but you have been travelling the last few days, and I daresay would like to go to bed.'

As a matter of fact, we were both desperately tired, and needed no rocking in the luxurious beds to which we were soon consigned. Our rooms opened into each other, and the last words I heard William say were,—

'For a silent man, he DOES blow certainly, but he's far better company than half the men you meet at home; and I like him.' And William Penrose by no means liked everybody.

CHAPTER X.

WE GO TO BALTIMORE.

'At morning and at evening both
   You merry were and glad,
So little care of sleepe and sloth
   These prettie ladies had.
When Tom came from labour,
   Or Ciss to milking rose,
Then merrily went their tabour,
   And nimbly went their toes.'

THE next morning, when William had had
his bath, which American civilisation had
long found a necessity, he confided to me,
in his delightfully innocent manner, which
often reminded me of his mother, that he
had fallen in love with Ella Pike, to which
I replied that I had sustained exactly the

same accident in regard to Angelina. We both agreed that they were charming girls, and that our prospect of the visit to Baltimore, before we did any further touring, was likely to prove very pleasant. At our age everything was easy, and we could return from Baltimore to Philadelphia, or, for the matter of hat, 'from any one given point to another,' as Euclid puts it. The given point, however, on this bright autumn morning, was clearly the stables, whither our host, whose silence was a thing of the past, conducted us, after a breakfast of which I still have tender memory. The young ladies did not accompany us, and the Greek Chorus was obviously no longer a necessity. Much had been explained; and Mr Buer was quite ready now to explain the rest. Nothing could exceed the luxurious arrangements of the stables, which covered a large extent of ground. Our host's breeding establishment was some miles off; but he had a number of horses of whom he had the highest possible opinion, but all without pedigrees. I confess I was glad to find William Penrose, who always understood horses, agreed with me that they were a poor lot, from the English point of view of horse flesh. What astonished me most were the wheels. Mr Buer had no less than thirty-seven carriages in his stables; and when he had his house full of company, carriages were being ordered to come round at all hours of the day and evening. When I thought of my experiences in Grosvenor Street, and English country houses,—of the care bestowed on the family barouche, and the three or four horses in the stables, and station dogcart,

I could not help marvelling at this display. The convenience of this plethora of conveyances was almost immediately demonstrated. Three phaetons were ordered out, and in one of them I soon found myself bowling out of the park gate. I absolutely refused to drive ; so one of the numerous stable-boys got on the box, and beside him sat one of the Miss Buers, while behind, in a roomy seat, sat Miss Angelina Pike and your humble servant. It was a most convenient happy arrangement for me. William started in a similar carriage, but was too independent to be driven, depending on the instructions of Miss Ella for his route.

'I suppose,' said Miss Angelina, 'you English don't drive out like this before lunch, and without any chaperon. There's no fun in walking in this sun, so why not drive ? Aunt Mary always drives to the farm in the morning, when she's staying here, and don't want us girls.'

'And I'm very glad Miss Buer takes that view.'

'Don't you like Aunt Mary ?' said her niece, in rather a piqued tone.

'Of course ; she is a charming old lady —only it's so much nicer to have you two girls to myself.'

'Wait till you get to Baltimore,' said Miss Pike, 'and see my cousin Lena, and then you won't think so much of us.'

Baltimore seemed the El Dorado of these young ladies, and until one arrived at that haven of the blest, clearly one had seen nothing. Moreover, Miss Ella Pike did not evidently care for flirtation just now, though perhaps she might later on do so, as she seemed to insinuate, at Baltimore.

I mentally resolved to push on to Baltimore.

'I wish you had been here earlier, for the corn. It looked so beautiful two months ago. All these fields about here were covered with it, and it is the grandest crop we grow. You had some corn last night for dinner. Did you like it?'

'Delicious,' I thought; 'when served as a vegetable with the *rôti*.'

'The squirrels do a lot of damage about here,' she observed; 'they want thinning in this part, as they devour the corn; but uncle has a weak side, and he can't bear to have the squirrels killed. Did you ever taste squirrel pie? Down in Kentucky, it's one of their prime dishes.'

'I should think it would take a great many squirrels to make a good pie, Miss Pike.'

'Depends on the size of the squirrel. You should see our squirrels in the park at Baltimore.'

The drive was a lovely one, nearly all the way following the route of the Hudson, on hilly ground, with the heights which surround Westpoint as a distant view. It was very delightful in the still, clear air of a late American fall ; but American young ladies, so far as my experience goes, do not care for scenery, except as they care for the decoration of their rooms, and that excludes sentiment. We drove home by another route, and arrived there in time for a sumptuous luncheon at two o'clock. If the American lady is a little deficient in romance, like many English beauties, she is not so in appetite.

Ne croyez pas qu'elle est ange. Point de tout ; elle mange les côtelettes, et elle lève

tous les matins à huits heures,—a brutal
sentiment, for which, though not my own,
I apologise. But the young ladies at Mr
Buer's hospitable house would not have
demanded an apology. They did not
seem to consider themselves angels, and
they greatly enjoyed their luncheon. In
the afternoon, time being allowed for a
possible siesta, or for a cigar, horses and
carriages came round once more, and once
more William and I were the esquires of
the two Miss Pikes ; but on this occasion,
on horseback, and with the chaperonage of
our host. The Miss Pikes were fair horse-
women, Miss Ella's small compact figure
showing to better advantage, perhaps, than
the more redundant charms of her sister,
on a horse ; but they both were in the
highest of spirits, and we were a merry
party. On our way we passed a magnifi-

cent red-brick building, surrounded with a good deal of well-cultivated land; and I asked Pike what it was.

'A Catholic College, founded here a few years ago by the Jesuits,' he replied. 'People in Europe don't know what the Jesuits are doing in this country; as they always have done, since the days of Loyola, they are advancing cautiously, and with consummate tact; but they *are* advancing, you bet, in spite of the Atheism and Freethinking in this country; and as long as they don't mix themselves up with our political institutions, I wish them success.'

It is extraordinary how liberal-minded, on religious matters, intelligent Americans nearly always are.

Our time in America was limited, and though we were pressed to stay on with

the Buers, and were greatly interested by
all we saw, we determined to go on to
Baltimore, after our three days' visit. I
will not say that the intended departure
for the same city of the Miss Pikes did
not partly influence us; but there was
much to be seen and done in the comparatively short time at our command;
and we parted from our kind host, pro-
mising to visit him later in New York.
With the young ladies, our farewell was
only a short *au revoir*, as they themselves
would be in Baltimore soon after we
arrived. They gave us their parents'
address. Miss Angelina assured us her
brother would make us members of the
Maryland Club, and that we should find
plenty of gaiety going on.

Some remark of mine to William, on
our journey, as to the interest Canon Caryl

would take in what we had heard about the Jesuits in America, led him to think a good deal of his mother, and of the possibility of having letters from her forwarded from New York. I thought he seemed, for the first time, a little depressed, as he remembered the great distance dividing them. I suppose the traveller, like the sailor, should be a light-hearted man, '*sans famille ;*' otherwise, if there is a mother, or a wife, or a sweetheart, as the sun goes down, *surgit amari aliquid.* But in due course we arrived at Baltimore, famous for its monuments, and its pretty girls. I remember someone saying, years ago, to me, after visiting Leamington, 'that it seemed to be all fly-men, and old women.' The first morning we strolled about Baltimore, we concluded that the monuments were very over-rated, and that the

pretty girls, apparently, stayed indoors, or
reserved themselves for that sitting out
on the door-steps, which, in warm weather,
is a custom peculiar to Baltimore. The
fact is, we Oxonians were not well-read
in American history, except so far as Lord
Chatham and Lord North were concerned.
The monuments and statues required explanation ; for the names inscribed thereon
sounded strange and unknown to us. I
have, however, noticed the same ignor-
ance as to former local celebrities among
Americans themselves. That evening, we
both received intimation that we were
elected honorary members of the Maryland Club, and also invitations to a ball
to be shortly given by Mrs John Pike,
and which was to commence at the extremely sensible hour of nine o'clock. I
have been, naturally, present at hundreds

of balls since this particular one, which was given in a house utterly unsuited for such an entertainment, the houses at Baltimore being mostly of very ordinary pretension; nevertheless, it is likely, as the reader will hereafter perceive, if he honours these pages by perusing them to the end, that it is *the* one ball I am never likely to forget.

Mrs John Pike was the sister, as already said, of Mr Buer, our late host; but she had not the refinement of manner of her brother, and she had never crossed the ocean. She was very proud of her daughter Angelina, as she well might be, and very anxious to take her to Paris and London; but Mr John Pike declined, at present, to advance funds for that purpose, and gave, as a reason, the then unsettled state of Europe. But Mrs Pike

only bided her time. She was a tuft-
hunter of the truest breed, and no Baltimore
young man should carry off, if she could
help it, the fine fortune and attractive
charms of her Angelina. All this, she
conveyed, not very indirectly, to William
and myself. The night of her ball, she
was attired as an English mother, on such
an occasion, at that time, would have
been, except for her magnificent diamonds,
which a duchess might have envied, and
which quite eclipsed my recollections of
Lady Duncan's display. Her hair, I recollect, was powdered, and a gorgeous
bird of fabulous origin constituted her
head-dress. I had full opportunity of ad-
miring it, as she insisted on taking me
herself in to supper, after dancing a square
dance with me. As William afterwards
remarked, 'The old girl has taken you

regularly in hand, and means to let you see what Baltimore can do.'

As we sat down together to a supper which was singularly homely, according to modern notions, I lifted my eyes, to see opposite to me one of the most lovely faces I ever beheld. She was very fair, with an exquisite skin, and the most beautiful golden hair. Her large limpid blue eyes, heavily and darkly lashed, seemed to gaze into space with a poetical languor, which contrasted with her vigorous frame, clothed in the purest white. Her voice, as she spoke to her companion, was in consonance with her beauty, low and distinct, like exquisite music ; her nose was ever so little *retroussé;* but her lips were full and red, her mouth small and refined, and her teeth, when she smiled, as she seemed to do whenever she spoke, were

like dazzling pearls. I turned at once to
Mrs Pike, 'Who is that lovely girl?'
Now, if Mrs Pike had been an English-
woman, she would have resented the
question, and, having a marriageable
daughter, although I had already impressed her with my own ineligibility,
she would have spoken slightingly of this
Venus of the ballroom.

'She is one of our Baltimore belles,—
Miss M'Carthy, an only daughter; and
her father, old M'Carthy, left a lot of
money. She and her mother will go to
Europe one day, and I guess they'll make
a pretty strong sensation over there.'

'Will you present me to her after
supper?'

Mrs Pike most good-naturedly promised she would, and shortly afterwards,
as we went upstairs, fulfilled her promise.

The lovely Dora M'Carthy must have noticed my admiration, as she raised the most wonderful eyes in the world to mine, and, on my asking for a dance, assured me quite pathetically that every dance was already 'booked.' (I should have thought badly of the Baltimore mankind if it had been otherwise.)

'But you are a stranger, so let us start.'

In an instant we were whirling round the room, to the music of a most delicious waltz.   To this day I can hum the air; to this hour I recall the wild intoxication of resting my arm on her waist, and the perfume that seemed to distil from the glittering hair, and the witchery of her eyes, as she abandoned herself to my guidance.   I had hoped she would sit out the next dance with me, which was a piece of presumption on my part, but all such ideas were dispelled by a somewhat truculent young gentleman claiming my enchantress for the next dance. But, as morning broke, we did dance the Lancers together, and she introduced me afterwards to her mother, who cordially begged me to call upon them.

CHAPTER XI.

MISS DORA M'CARTHY.

'I pray, sir, tell me, is it possible that love should of
a sudden take such hold?'

WILLIAM and I walked home to our
hotel, beneath the brilliant rays of sun-
rise.

'I never spent,' said he, 'a more delightful night. Baltimore is a charming
place, and Ella Pike the nicest girl
I know. You seemed dancing with a
very pretty woman. What is her
name?'

'Miss Dora M'Carthy. I am going to call on her mother this afternoon.'

'The deuce you are! You promised to have a look at the duck shooting and decoys. I can't let you off that.'

'I shall call on the M'Carthys first,' I said, in what William always called my 'Huguenot' manner.

So he said no more, and we turned into bed.

'Well, my inconstant swain,' he said at luncheon, 'you're an awful fellow to travel with. You fall in love every day with some fresh beauty. It was only two days ago you were raving about the other Miss Pike.'

'I am not aware, William,' I said with dignity, 'that I am raving about anybody; and as you are going only on a visit of inspection on the important question of the ducks, I can't see that an hour's delay need put you out.'

'Nor shall it, you bet. I shall be found at the club, with a Havanna and a cool drink. So farewell, and good luck.'

As a usual thing, William would have accompanied me on such a visit, but to-day I preferred going alone. That afternoon, in the shady garden, sitting under the trees, I found the beautiful Dora, looking more bewitching than ever, in her coquettish, well-fitting, simple brown dress.

'The sun was still powerful, so I came out here to read,' she explained, pointing to her book. 'Ma has gone down town, but she'll be back directly, so pray sit down.'

It is almost impossible to propose marriage to a young lady of any nation after a
few hours' acquaintance, and if I had been
possessed of the effrontery to do so, I
should have richly deserved the point-
blank refusal which certainly would have
been my reward. Still, in my youthful
impetuosity, my devotion was very marked,
and I was duly that day enrolled amongst
the considerable band of Miss Dora's admirers. I now greatly rejoiced that, with
the love of independence natural to young
men, we had betaken ourselves to an hotel
at Baltimore, instead of availing ourselves
of Mr Pike's hospitality. Consequently,
being perfectly free, and Miss M'Carthy
being allowed by her mother a vast deal
of liberty also, scarcely a day passed that
we did not meet; and, as the society at
Baltimore is extremely small, we nearly

always met again in the evening. William watched our growing intimacy with rather an anxious eye. I think he remembered his conversation with his mother the evening we settled to start on this journey, and he felt a little weighted with responsibility. As the days wore on, he hinted that we were spending a most unequal division of our time at Baltimore, as, indeed, we had already been there three weeks. Looking back on that time, I see that he was, as always, most unselfish and forbearing; whereas I had completely become a slave to the beautiful Dora, and in that slavery for a short time forgot my friend.

At last one morning, when the weather was bitterly cold, and some signs of a snow-storm were apparent, he said, rather gravely,—

'My dear Clare, you really must pull

yourself together a little, or I shall have
to leave you here alone.   As it is, we are
bound to exceed our three months' absence, and I cannot leave my mother, and
all the business at Carnaby, for an inter-
minable time.'

I clasped his hand.   We should always
be dear friends till the end.

'Give me till Friday (it was Wednesday morning), and we will go to Washington on Friday.'

So it was agreed between us.   He
added,—

'You must not be angry with me, or
think I want to lecture you because I am
older ; but, if you take my advice, you
won't enter upon any serious matter
with Miss M'Carthy between this and
Friday.   She   will   be   coming   to
Europe   next   summer,   and   then   you

can decide whether to speak to her or not.'

I only nodded in a mysterious way, and left the room. That afternoon I was engaged to drive with Miss M'Carthy, in the beautiful park outside the city. How lovely she looked in her fur cap and cloak!—the keen air bringing colour to her cheeks as she handled the ribbons, and we bowled along together towards the park. By some lucky coincidence, she had not brought a groom, and I gladly got down to open the one or two gates we came to, long since removed. Her golden hair was flying over her face, beaming with animation. I never, at any period of her life, saw her look so handsome, or carry herself so proudly, as she did that afternoon.

'Look at the squirrels!' she said, as the little grey creatures, aroused by the clatter of our steeds, took refuge in the trees. 'Poor little beasts! they are in for a fall of snow. How stupid you are this afternoon, Mr Strong! What is the matter with you?'

'The matter is, I have to go away to Washington, and continue our tour, on Friday, and I don't like going at all.'

'And why not? It certainly is rather cold weather for moving about; but you will see Niagara, no doubt, in its grandest dress of ice and snow. If I was you, I should be delighted to move on.

'I don't think you would,' I said slowly. 'The fact is, since I have known you, Baltimore has become very dear to me.'

In a moment her gaiety vanished, and a shade of sadness crossed her beautiful face.

'My dear boy, you must not think of anything serious, at your age. When we come to England next year, you will have seen more, and thought more. You cannot know your own mind yet about Baltimore or anything else. But I am glad you like my dear Baltimore, and that you also like me, a little.'

Somehow, her muff tumbled off her knees, and, somehow—I shall never feel quite sure how—our lips met, and that was my only love-passage with Dora M'Carthy. No doubt, Mrs Grundy will think it a vulgar one, and that Miss M'Carthy was a forward baggage, and I an impertinent young man. *Soit.* I take this occasion to say I never did, and I never shall, care much for Mrs Grundy's opinion on any subject whatever. Dora whipped up her horses immediately after this incident, and talked volubly, as the snow-flakes fell, and as we drove towards home, without any further sentimental allusion to my departure.

'My grandfather was an Irishman,—came over here from the county Tyrone, without a dollar; but he joined a friend out here, and made a pile. I should like to go to Ireland. My father was born there; but they were only small farmers, who tried the new country. There are not many Irish in Baltimore. You have met C—, he claims an Irish peerage. At least, he says he could do so. We are nearly all what you call

Tories in Baltimore. Well, good-bye! We shall meet to-night and, of course, you and your friend must dine with ma and me to-morrow night.'

'Thank you very much,' I said; 'of course, we shall be delighted to come; and you have promised me two dances to-night.'

'There will be a suicide if I give you more.'

Her tall stately figure passed up the stone steps, and there was no more to be said. William never asked me any questions, though he knew how the afternoon had been spent; and he at once agreed to eat our last dinner at Baltimore with the M'Carthys, though I knew he would rather have done so at the Pikes' house, where Ella remained, to his more constant and

better-regulated mind, a˙ lasting mag-
net.

At the dance that night, with the
perfume of her lips still lingering on
mine, after that friendly salutation (for
it was not a lover's kiss), I passed
one more delightful evening. The next
day was a sad one to me. William,
though sorry to leave the Pike family,
and specially the younger daughter of
the house, had satiated himself for
weeks with slaughter of the ducks, and
was full of reflection on the passage
of the time. On the whole, he was
glad to leave Baltimore. That last
evening, Dora and I had no opportunity for a *tête-à-tête* until, just as
we left, she beckoned me into the
boudoir.

'We might meet in New York; but I

don't, somehow, think we shall. But, anyhow, I hope you've had a good time ; and
when we come to Europe, ma will let you
know.'

Her tiny, diamond-ringed hand was
clasped in mine, and, for the time, the
most lovely woman I have ever known
was lost sight of by me, though, often and
often, during the succeeding weeks, I saw
her face in my dreams. I had nothing but
those dreams, and that one kiss, to remind
me of her. And, as for myself, I think
it probable now, that 'out of sight was
out of mind.' We were destined, however, to meet and to part again.

Onward we went to Washington, only,
comparatively, a trivial journey ; and there
the gaieties were at their height. An old
Etonian was in the Embassy—a great personal friend of William's ; and, of course, we

carried a letter to our Minister. But with
my departure from Miss M'Carthy's presence, my interest in society seemed, for the
present, to vanish; and so, after a week, we
went on our way. I have no intention of
assuming a guide-book literary style, so
shall content myself by saying that, both
on this first occasion and on subsequent
visits to the States, I thought Philadelphia
the brightest and the nicest city in
America. I know no shops, and no
thoroughfares, so bright and gay, both by
day and night, as those of the old Quaker
city. Chestnut Street is a thoroughly
cheery promenade, far more so than any
street in New York, and, to my ideas, than
any in the almighty Boston, with all its
social and literary pretensions,—the one city
in America which always reminds me of a
big provincial town in England. But, no

doubt, then I was in a discontented state of mind, and it is a true remark to say that one's views of men and things depend on the condition of one's own mental and physical being. Dora M'Carthy had much to answer for. I brooded on, and must have been a deplorable fellow-traveller to my dear friend; but he understood all the circumstances, and never said one word of reproach.

We saw Niagara under most favourable circumstances, for the time of year, for there was a brilliant sun shining the morning we issued from the Clifton House, and the icicles and blocks of ice were magnificent, with the foam rising up in clouds, and its gorgeous prismatic colours. Niagara was not then vulgarised, and it was possible to observe all the different effects

without the intervention of touts, and the
presence of excursionists, and perpendi-
cular tram lines.   Yet it never can be
totally degraded by any surroundings,
however coarse and mercenary; and I
pity the man or woman who can gaze
at that mysterious and terrible whirlpool
below the rapids without a feeling of awe
in thinking of the one side of Nature
which is pitiless and ghastly—its immut-
ability among all the 'chances and changes
of this mortal life.'   The whirlpool at
Niagara will still be making its fatal
and profound eddies when the greatest
minds of the world, and what they wrote,
are buried in oblivion.

Years afterwards I saw Niagara in a
brilliant September night, with a harvest
moon shining grandly over the troubled
waters.   'O God!' I prayed, 'take

me to Thyself in Thine own good time, and without a weary struggle. Beyond these waters, and this cold judicial moon, there must be rest and eternal peace.'

CHAPTER XII.

A STRANGE SITUATION.

'Oh, may we all for death prepare!
    What has he left? and who's his heir?'

WILLIAM PENROSE and I had been absent from England six months, instead of three, when we stepped on shore from the tender at the Liverpool landing-place. A week before sailing for England, we had directed all letters to be sent to us at Liverpool, as we should rest there a night before proceeding to Carnaby. William had found a note from his mother, in New York, just before we sailed, addressed to us both jointly.

'CARNABY MANOR.

'MY DEAR BOYS,—I am glad to hear, at last, you are turning your steps to New York, with a view to coming home; because, of course, I pine a little, every now and then, to see you. Not that I am lonely; for in London I was quite gay, for me; and Christmas Day I spent with the Chamiers, who had a very festive party; but I thought much of you both. Since I have been at Carnaby, I have had constant visitors. Mr Eardley is here now. You will have heard he is now in Parliament, and seems to be rising rapidly in public estimation. We shall see how he succeeds. For myself, I think he will do great things; but he is on the

wrong side. I was delighted at Clare's
description of Niagara ; but he must not
take the melancholy side of life too much
to heart, at his early stage of life. I am
glad you have both, so far as I know, not
lost your hearts to any American enchantress; and I long to hear all your
adventures, especially William's ideas of
sport in the States. I suppose he greatly
enjoyed the duck-shooting. Tim rides
Roderick vigorously every day; but the
stables want looking after, and their
master's presence will be a very desirable
event. I am sorry you did not care for your
literary friends in Boston, as I delight in
the little I know of American fiction ; but
not in their poetry. Every morning I hope
to find a letter fixing the week of your return ; but I shall wait here patiently, and
not allow my maternal instincts to bring

me to Liverpool in this very bitter English spring. I was at Elcote a few days ago, and heard Lord Francis was dying. . . . —Ever yours,

'MARY PENROSE.'

I also found a letter, among others, which caused my heart to beat very fast. It was curious that, throughout the voyage home, I had felt a strange presentiment of coming disaster. Of course, my gloom was attributed by William to the feeling which had rather darkened my latter stay in the States; but, in reality, it was some vague sense of an important epoch in my life. When I had read General Rosemere's letter, at the Liverpool Hotel, I believed in my presentiment, and, though far from superstitious, few events of importance have occurred to me through life, without a previous foreboding. The letter was a short one, and ran in the following terms.

'DEAR CLARE,—I hear you have directed your letters to be sent to Liverpool, and that you are expected there for a night some time in the course of next week. It is very important that I should see you as soon as possible after your arrival in England. I to-day attended the funeral of poor old Lord Francis Sherlock, in the capacity, to my great surprise, of his sole executor. He had been ill for some weeks, but absolutely refused to see any of his relations or old friends, including myself. His will was produced by the family law-yers, and by it you are largely benefited. He has left you back, absolutely, your

grandmother's diamonds. He has also
left you Elcote, and Lady Duncan's eighty
thousand pounds, fettered with the extraordinary condition that you are to lose
both one and the other on your marriage.
If you remain a bachelor, you can bequeath
both the estate and the funded property,
which is placed in the hands of trustees.
If you marry, all passes, with Sherlock
and the whole of his fortune (excepting
a jointure left to a lady), to his nephew,
the Duke of Sutham's second son. This
is about as plainly as I can state the case,
but you must see me at once, and peruse
the will; and there will be much to explain. We ought to meet at Sherlock
first. Will you therefore let me know
at once on your landing what day will
suit you to dine and sleep at Sherlock?
Northampton is the nearest town, as you

probably know.   The only inmate at
Sherlock is the lady in question; but the
place does not pass to the heir for six
months, and all the Elcote papers are
there.   I am glad Sherlock has reversed
the unjust will of Lady Duncan, though
his peculiar views on matrimony may, I
fear, not entirely fall in with your own.
Ever yours,   JACK ROSEMERE.'

To say that I was thunderstruck, as the
colloquial phrase goes, on reading this
letter but inadequately describes my state
of mind.   It appeared to me that Lord
Francis had revenged himself, by this
extraordinary disposition to me, fettered
with such a cruel condition, for my refusal to accept the hand of friendship he
offered soon after my grandmother's death.
I do not think so now in later years, but

such was my not unnatural conclusion at that time.

On descending to our dinner in the coffee-room, I ordered a bottle of champagne, and silently handed William this letter to read. To my surprise, he, who had such control, when he chose, over his mental emotions, gave way entirely to his sense of the injustice which two wills, executed by persons both between eighty and ninety years of age, brought upon me.

' If ever I get into Parliament,' he said, ' I will bring in a bill to render all wills executed after the testator has passed seventy-five years, void and illegal.'

I could not forbear laughing.

' I suppose some people would envy me, and say I was uncommonly lucky. To come into three thousand a year, and a beautiful old manor house, exactly adapted for such a moderate income, is not a calamity, William, if it were not for the fiendish provision, which, of course, I shall some day bring into force.'

'Listen to me, Clare. Anyhow, marriage for you yet would be a mistake. With your abilities, and this fortune, and position in the county, added to your own, you must seek a career—a political career. Even I intend to do so some day. Your early marriage would cripple you. So, for the present, I should forget altogether the condition on which you inherit. Time enough ten years hence to consider it, and its bearings on your happiness. Anyhow, you have the diamonds.'

'Which, with a cynicism worthy of Lord Francis, I can bestow on any woman in the world who is not my wife.'

' True ; but, for the present, I should keep them for myself at Coutts' Bank.'

There was an insincere ring in my dear friend's consolation. I knew quite well that he felt that all my future happiness was necessarily risked by this second will. Sensational accounts would be sure to be spread as to my inheritance, throughout the county; and the man who was made rich by it, so long as he remained a bachelor, was invited either to shut himself out from his own natural instincts for home and love, or beckoned—as, perchance, Lord Francis wished—to the life which he had himself notoriously led for many years. We both agreed, however, that the first thing for me to do was to go, as General Rosemere wished, to Sherlock for a night. So I sent off a letter at once to the

General, to say I would arrive at Sherlock the day after he would receive my
note.

'We can go to Carnaby to-morrow
morning, as I think my mother would be
hurt if you did not come with me first to
her. You know her romantic nature.
Then the next day you can go to Sherlock, and find out exactly how you stand,
from Rosemere.'

I could not sleep that night, and I sat
by my open bedroom window, gazing out
on a clear, bright sky, and a watery moon,
and dreaming over my possible future, and
my strange, present position. Upward
floated the sounds of revelry from the
Liverpool streets—the strange snatches of
music, old familiar airs, fraught with a
pathos, amid the mass of humanity, struggling in their sleepless effort for pleasure

and amusement, as the night wore on. Sailors were having their 'last fling' on shore; sin, and misery, and death were around me, all rendered more melancholy by the fitful bursts of merriment, the drunken laughter, and the boisterous cries of a seaport town at night.

What a medley it all was! what a puzzle this short mysterious existence! When 'life's fitful fever' shall be over, shall we not wonder at the great interest it has caused us, and at the passions, the tears, and the hopes it has excited? I felt an eagerness to know my end. How would all this change in my fortunes affect this life, for which I professed so keen a contempt, and where, at last, should I succumb to the mortal agony, which Bacon conjectured was no more bitter than the effort to struggle into existence?

But the solemn tone of some church bell warned me that another day would soon be breaking, and that an ample bed, un-rocked by waves, invited repose.

CHAPTER XIII.

MY NEW INHERITANCE.

'Amour folie aimable :
Ambition sottise sérieuse.'

I MUST not linger on our coming home.
It was a repetition to William of many
happy 'comings home' from school, from
college, and from bachelor wanderings.
Happy those who can recall in after life
such greetings! and I, who had not been
so fortunate in the bygone years, was
folded in the arms of my dear, faithful,
loving friend once more.

'Welcome! dear Clare,' she said, as
she led me across the hall into her own

pet sanctum. William had rushed off into the gardens, and to visit the stables,
and the farm, and the dairy, where all his
friends, human and animal, were eagerly
awaiting his arrival.

She took both my hands, and kissed
me.

'My dear boy, I have heard about the
will, and I cannot find words to say all I
think about it. But I know your nature
well enough to be certain you won't allow
your life to be sacrificed, hereafter, for a
few paltry thousands a year. Only wait;
and be sure you fix on somebody, when
you *do* think on marrying, worthy of the
great sacrifice you will make for her. For
Elcote will be a sacrifice for any man to
surrender. But you are young; and, so
far from believing in the 'vita brevis,' it
seems to me a very long affair; and you

have plenty of time to consider. You will
go to Sherlock, I suppose, at once?'

'To-morrow. I have written to General
Rosemere that I will meet him at dinner-
time, to-morrow. There are a few points
to clear up, and Rosemere is sole executor.'

'Have you thought what you would like
to do at present?'

'I have scarcely had time; but I suppose I must take chambers in London in
any case; and I should like to move most
of my things to Elcote. It would be so
nice to live near you and William
here.'

That evening, as we three sat alone together after dinner, Mrs Penrose said,—

'Now, William, tell Clare about the letter
you have found here from Mr Eardley.'

'You had better read it, my dear
fellow.'

It was an offer of Mr Eardley to make
him his private secretary, with a view to
a start in learning politics, and possibly,
later on, as the writer hinted, some insight
into official life.

'They say,' said William's mother,
'that he has every chance, if the present Government go out, of obtaining
some minor post in the next administration; and as William takes the Liberal
side in politics, it may be a good opening.
I was brought up as a Tory; but your
father's family, William, as you know,
have always been Whigs.'

There was no doubt about it, that this
offer opened some sort of a future to
William, whose duties would probably, at
all events at present, be light, and whose
position and pecuniary prospects would fit
him later to stand for his own county, when

this secretaryship would have brought
him in contact with many political per-
sonages.

'You can always run down here,' said
his mother; 'and I shall remain longer
in Devonshire Place than I have done of
late years.'

William kissed his mother, and said,—

'Of course, I will write to Eardley, and
gratefully accept the post of scribe. I
don't myself believe he is a Radical in
politics, only in philosophy; and office
will tone down even his philosophy, if
he gets it.'

I rejoiced at these good tidings, and at
the prospect for my old friend. It was
better than coming into an immediate
fortune, with such fetters as were im-
posed on me.

The next evening—a boisterous and

rough one, which led me to appreciate
the advantages of *terra firma*—I found
myself the sole occupant of a ridiculous
landau, which had been sent to meet me
at Northampton, and which now, at a
very leisurely pace, under the guidance
of an ancient and time-ridden Jehu, conducted me, in solitary grandeur, through
narrow roads to one of the lodges of
Sherlock Park. I had, of course, donned
the conventional mourning for Lord
Francis. He had bequeathed to me a
large fortune, and, though I felt no
sorrow for his death, my Grosvenor Street
education prescribed my apparel on this
occasion.

Sherlock is the finest Tudor mansion in
the Midlands; and it would be clearly
superfluous for me here to enter into a
long account of its unrivalled beauties of

external architecture, especially as I never visited the place except upon this one occasion, and it certainly is improbable that I shall ever see it again. Built entirely of brick, with stone decorations, it covers an immense area, and lies in a hollow of the magnificent deer park which surrounds it,—a wooded hill rising before the principle façade, which thus prevents any distant view. After a drive from the lodge gate we had entered, of nearly two miles, through very undulating ground, and superb trees, we arrived at the famous cedar avenue, which is perfectly straight, and at the end of which stands the house. For many, many years this beautiful place had been closed to the county and society. Antiquarians came and rhapsodied on its loveliness, tourists came on the one day a week when some

of the state-rooms were open for
inspection, and artists lingered in the
superb gallery, containing the pictures
which have since been disposed of at a
public auction by Lord Francis's successor.
Whatever his peculiarities and delin-
quencies, Lord Francis would have shud-
dered at the idea of those pictures—which
had been collected in Queen Anne's reign
by his maternal ancestor,—the friend of
Harley and Bolingbroke,—the patron of
Pope and of Addison—being appraised
in a London auctioneer's room. I was
ushered through the hall, and a suite of
many beautiful apartments, into the
saloon, a room perfectly octagonal, in the
centre of the house, where a fire, burning
brightly, threw its cheerful light on the
massive gilding and somewhat florid
decorations of this, the smallest recep-

tion-room of the house. The old butler, who himself conducted me to the room, with an obsequiousness which betokened a knowledge of my position in his late master's will, and who eyed me with well-bred curiosity, remarked, in a solemn tone, that he would inform General Rosemere I had arrived. The General came on the scene almost immediately, and shook me warmly by the hand.

'So glad you managed to come. I wanted to get the lawyer here, too, to-night; but he could not leave town. But, after dinner, we can go through what is necessary ; and I thought we would sit here until we move into the smoking-room. The rooms are so vast and dreary for only two persons to sit in; though poor Sherlock, when he was here, always sat in the library.'

Dinner was announced, and we both felt an uncomfortable pang as we took our long walk through rooms, all half lighted, into the dining-room, a magnificent apartment, mostly in darkness, but in the centre of which a small round table, covered with wax lights, and glittering with old silver, invited us to our meal. While the servants remained in the room, our conversation was, necessarily, conventional, and chiefly respecting my recent visit to America. General Rosemere, a thorough man of the world, was fairly intelligent, had seen much, and read much, and was as well acquainted with the brilliant as with what has been· called ' the seamy' side of life. The dinner was, I remember, exactly what I thought then, and think still, a dinner should be. It was obviously cooked by a French *chef*, and in the old style of French cooking. It was just sufficient for two men, and included, of course, the delicacies of the hour ; but one did not feel wearied by long courses, and unnecessary *entrées*. Lord Francis had well drilled all his servants ; and, as for the wine after dinner, it would have been hard to assign the palm to the Lafitte, the Closvongeot, or the Madeira, which last quite eclipsed any wine I drank in America.

I could not help saying,—'We feast magnificently in the dead man's house,' when we were left alone.

The General shrugged his shoulders.

'Ah yes ! Poor Sherlock ! If any man ever understood comfort, he did ; and the Duke's son inherits a magnificent cellar. He was here yesterday,—in fact, is here constantly. He seems to me a poor sort of fellow. Sherlock never would see him in his lifetime; and latterly, since your grandmother's death, he always spoke rather bitterly of you. So his will surprised me, and specially in the matter of my executorship. What do you say to your good fortune, Clare?'

'Well, after all, my grandmother's fortune was left from me most unjustly, and now that it comes back to me, it comes back with a provision which makes it nearly worthless.'

'Don't say that,' he interposed hurriedly. 'Keep out of marriage; in nine cases out of ten, it is a fatal mistake.'

As General Rosemere was now married, I was a little amused at this view, but did not wish to discuss it with him.

'I suppose,' I said, 'you will prove the

will at once. There is no difficulty of
any sort.'

'None. There are very few legatees.
His nephew is the residuary legatee. He
leaves me five thousand pounds. He
leaves you, as you know, the fortune of
your grandmother, and Elcote, on the condition of non-marriage. If you marry,
his nephew inherits all. He leaves you
absolutely Lady Duncan's diamonds, and
her miniature, which, I think, I forgot to
mention. It is a large miniature, by
Cosway, and set in brilliants. The diamonds are at Coutts' Bank, and you will
have them as soon as the will is proved.
The miniature is here, and you can take it
away to-morrow. Of course, there are
legacies to a good many of his dependants
here; and a large annuity is given to a
lady, who has lived here for some years.

But there is a copy of the will, which has been made for you, and which you can also take away. I want you to go to London, to-morrow, and, as soon as possible, see the lawyers about Elcote. The papers, which are very voluminous, concerning the manor of Elcote, have always been kept here ; but now they should be deposited, when probate is granted, with your own lawyers.'

Nothing could be more clear or straightforward than General Rosemere's statement to me ; and it seemed that Lord Francis could have chosen no better executor,—as he had decided, with his usual eccentricity, to have only one for the administration of so large a property. In this view, I found later, in the smoking-room, I was mistaken, as Lord Francis, it appeared, had named his elder brother, the

Duke, as the General's co-executor; but his Grace had renounced, on hearing that Elcote was left away to me. General Rosemere had forgotten accidentally to mention this to me. I asked him, as we smoked our cigars, what the Duke had said, and if he had attended the funeral.

'Oh, yes, he came here, and seemed greatly interested in the place, which, he said, he had not seen for twenty-five years. When he heard about Elcote he whistled, and uttered a prolonged and guttural " D—n." Then he asked what sort of a fellow you were. " Tell him from me," he said, "I wish to know him; and, if he comes to Southam, I will ask all the most beautiful women in England to tempt him; only they will have to be virtuous as well as beautiful, and there will be the difficulty.'

He went away the same afternoon, after the will was read.'

'And what about the lady here? Is she still in the house?'

'Mrs Adeane is still here. She has lived for years in a separate wing of the house, the furthest removed from the rooms Lord Francis used. He has left her an annuity of a thousand a year, and as she is still young, and remarkably handsome, she will probably marry well. By-the-bye, she expressed a wish to see you, before you leave to-morrow; but, of course, you can do as you like about that.'

'Oh! by all means, I will see her, if she sends me a message,' I replied; for I was not altogether free from curiosity about this mysterious lady. I was very glad to find, later on, that the General's and my

bedrooms were close to each other. There
was a stillness and a gloom about this vast
house, with its innumerable galleries and
passages, which rather chilled one. But I
saw no ghost; although there is said to be
one at Sherlock, in the haunted room;
and I slept profoundly until my shutters
were opened, and a bright spring sun
poured its rays upon my bed.

After breakfast, General Rosemere produced the miniature of my grandmother.
and handed it to me. It was a large oval
picture, set in a gold case, and surrounded
with brilliants. She must have been about
thirty years of age when it was painted;
and it was a beautiful work of art. Her
hair was powdered, and drawn back
with two large curls, one on each side;
a red rose was its only adorn-
ment; the lacework on her bosom, or

'modesty,' was tied with pale blue ribbons.

'He told me once,' said General Rosemere, 'she was the only woman in his whole life he ever wished to marry, and that she was twelve years older than himself.'

'She must have been, there is no doubt, a very lovely woman ; and for my father's sake,' I added, 'I am very glad to have this, and shall regard it as an heir-loom.'

At that moment a footman entered the room and asked, with Mrs Adeane's com-pliments, if it would be convenient to me to call on her now. I at once followed him, with a glance at the General, and found myself exploring an entirely new (to me) part of the house. I was ushered into a boudoir, which bore signs of much

taste and refinement, and which seemed
even overcrowded with valuable china;
but had scarcely had time to survey my
surroundings, when Mrs Adeane entered,
dressed in the deepest crape. She was
a very striking woman, as much from her
tall, commanding figure as from her features, which were classically beautiful, though
not of a soft or an appealing type. She
held out her hand, with a slight smile, and,
motioning me to a chair, said, in a very
gentle voice,—

'I am leaving Sherlock to-morrow, and,
after all Lord Francis has said to me of
you, I thought I might venture to make
your acquaintance, though it is unlikely
that we shall ever meet again.'

'I am sure,' I said, 'I am delighted and
flattered beyond words at your message;
but, I am afraid, anything poor Lord

Francis said of me in his lifetime, was
not complimentary.'

'I assure you, you are mistaken. He
always spoke of you with tenderness, almost, as the only descendant of the woman
he had loved.'

'I have heard from others exactly the
contrary.'

'Possibly; but it was to me, and perhaps to me only, that he really said what
he felt.'

'Then how do you explain the cruel
provision in his will? I suppose you are
aware how he has tried to ruin my
life.'

'Mr Strong, you misjudge him. He
has tried to save you from the misery
which marriage so often produces. If
you take his advice, as conveyed in his
will, you will not marry at all. You will

preserve your independence, and not run the hazard of a life of care, and anxiety, and responsibility. But, if you do not take his advice, at least he will have saved you from being married for your possessions,—hunted down by some scheming dowager,—treated as a question of 'chattels,' where love is not in the 'pool,' but where settlements, and an establishment, and ample pin money, are the only allurement. Lord Francis knew the world; and his will, to my mind, is a monument of worldly good judgment.'

She spoke calmly, but with wonderful decision, and certainly put things from a strange point of view; and I afterwards, in years to come, recalled what she had so cynically said. When we parted, she begged me to remember Lord Francis with kindness. 'He was in many ways eccentric, but he meant no harm to you.' I promised her I would, at all events, treasure up no ill feelings of any sort, and she answered, 'As the heir to Elcote, and four thousand a year, you ought to find it easy to be generous.'

She afterwards married an Irish baronet, and made him, I believe, an excellent wife; so she did not, in practice, carry out her theories as expressed to me about marriage. She was partially received within her own county in Ireland, and died, after many years of devotion to works of charity and religion.

I left for London, where I put up at an hotel, that afternoon; and on my journey fell to perusing the voluminous will which I carried with me, and in

which the following passage occurs :—' I
desire that my funeral be as decent
and private as possible, and in the
next churchyard to where I happen
to die.'

CHAPTER XIV.

I SETTLE IN LONDON.

'Dans le monde vous avez trois sortes d'amis :
Vos amis qui vous aiment : vos amis qui ne
Se soucient pas de vous : et vos amis
Qui vous haissent.'

DURING the time at my disposal in London, while searching for suitable chambers, and subsequently visiting innumerable shops, and occasionally rushing to Lord Francis's lawyers in the City, I often reflected on the not altogether creditable fact that, in the course of a brief two years, I had no less than three times imagined myself, rightly or wrongly, to have fallen in love. It certainly seemed a misfortune that a man whose wealth was held entirely on the tenure of celibacy, should, apparently, be so susceptible to female charms. There was my cousin, Ida de Chamier, there was Angelina Pike, there was Dora M'Carthy. The laws of England prohibited my marrying all three : Lord Francis's will declared I should marry nobody ; and it was extremely possible that not one of these young ladies would have married me, in any case, and certainly not under present circumstances. For I was a humble man, and could not imagine that I could be loved only for myself,—another result of my early training, in which the power of money had held so prominent a place. But a girl may, after all, very naturally hesitate to allow such a sacrifice as I was called upon to make in proposing marriage, and to dread the possibility of regret in after years, when the sacrifice has long been made. She may very fairly think, 'He is carried away now by his devotion to me; but some day he will look at things more calmly, and will call to mind that to win me he gave up his fortune and his beautiful old manor house: and then will come the suggestion,—'and perhaps, after all, it was too much to throw away.' My case seemed beset with difficulties, the more I considered it; so at last I gave up my thoughts to the furnishing of the handsome chambers I had taken in Piccadilly —the nicest situation in the world; for, after all, when one has travelled much, and seen all the great cities east and west, one comes back once more to Piccadilly; and whether from old association or not, I am not sure, but it remains the street most like home, the most familiar, and the best beloved.

The spring was advancing, Parliament was in session, and London was filling fast, though many families were in mourning, and it was certain that the season would not be a gay one. We were still plunged in that terrible war which cost us so many of our bravest sons, and in which the Guardsmen, idlers once in Piccadilly and Hyde Park, had done such prodigies of valour. But a certain outside gaiety must always be found in London as the spring advances, and the chestnut trees burst into blossom. Meanwhile, established in my delightful rooms, I found, but not to my surprise, that all my grandmother's friends, and their relatives and connections, began to be once more aware

of my existence. By this time, the contents of the will were known, and I
appeared as an eligible friend and acquaintance, if not, from the matronly point of
view, a possible *parti.* My hall table, on
my return in the evening, before dinner,
was always quite covered with cards and
notes, and, after a while, I began to be
amused with the excitement of going out
in the evening, and making new friends.
It was a new phase of life, as I had, since
Lady Duncan's death, entirely dropped
out of sight; but it was not one that
could ever have enthralled me for long,
and my really pleasant evenings were
spent in Devonshire Place, where Mrs
Penrose constantly had delightful literary
and musical *réunions.*

How often have I sat at her round
dinner-table, at that time, and enjoyed the

charm of listening to brilliant conversation, an art which is, I am told, almost extinct! How skilfully she would stimulate conversation, without ever appearing to lead it, and how dexterously, and apparently unconsciously, evoke the topics which showed her guests at their best!

Mr Eardley was very often there, perhaps a little more reserved than heretofore. He spoke always of William most enthusiastically. 'He was to stand at the next election for a certain borough, and he was sure to distinguish himself. How curious that such a brilliant man should have done so little at Oxford, and not even taken his degree!' To Mrs Penrose, you may imagine how sweet was all this, spoken as it was by an earnest, sincere man, who was rapidly making a name in the House of Commons, and in English

politics outside it. And, next to his mother,
the praise of Mr Eardley, and William's
own enthusiasm, was, perhaps, most welcome to me. If one's own life is marked
out on other lines, and distinction is not
one's destiny, the next best thing is to see
those you love succeed, and it was impossible not to see that William was gaining
rapidly the good opinions of those who
were best able to aid him in his political
career.

The De Chamiers were also often in
Devonshire Place, and I renewed my acquaintance with them, which soon ripened
into intimacy. Ida regained her ascen-
dency over my heart quickly, and, though
I never hinted at my admiration of her
beauty, we were, at all events, now firm
friends. She and her father often came to
my chambers to drink tea, and admire my

last new acquisitions in the way of prints
and *bric-à-brac*, and it was in contempla-
tion that, later on, when everyone was
leaving London, they would come and pay
me a little visit at Elcote, where I now
had a very modest establishment. Ida
had very much improved in her appearance and figure since I first saw her at
Carnaby, but had lost none of her delightful archness and vivacity. It was not,
however, even now, until people knew her
well, that they discovered her great intelligence, and how well her father had edu-
cated her bright, clear, intuitive mind. I
remember once hearing an Irish father
say that his girls were so pretty that the
only education he felt inclined to give them
was to enable them to ride straight across
country in the day time, and to dance
gracefully at night. But M. de Chamier

had taken a very different view of what a girl's education should be. In those days, the higher education of women—to use a vague but popular term—was not much discussed; and it was all the more to the credit of the man of business that he had found time to personally supervise his only child's education, and to form her taste. Mrs Penrose, for whom the talents of youth had always possessed a peculiar charm, had long known and appreciated my cousin Ida's abilities, and had, latterly, constantly lent her books of poetry and history, which her father's library in Bloomsbury did not contain. Though there was the same vivacity, there was, perhaps, at times, a shade of pensiveness which I did not recollect formerly, and which made her even more attractive in my eyes.

One night, I remember, I was dining in Devonshire Place with a small party of twelve, amongst whom were the De Chamiers and Canon Caryl, whose grave, shrewd conversation always interested me. He was no longer under the strict rules which formerly had bound him, and was now a great diner-out in London, among that most cliquish of all societies—the Catholic *beau monde* of London. Sitting by the side of our hostess, who, as usual, looked one's ideal of an elderly English lady, with her beautiful white hair, and expressive clever face, his austere features were lighted up almost with animation.

'And where is William to-night?' he asked.

'He was so sorry not to be here, and begged me to make his apologies to you: but, as you know, it is a great night at the House, and William went over from Whitehall at five o'clock, and

sent me a note to say it was quite un-
certain when he could get back here.'

'I thought probably he would go. I
hear Eardley is to speak to-night against
Reform. Only conceive Eardley seced-
ing from his party on such a question!
But he says education must come, in
his judgment, before further extension
of the franchise. If the Government are
beaten, they will resign ; and the quid-
nuncs say Eardley is sure of an Under-
Secretaryship in the new Ministry.'

'Did you hear,' asked Mrs Penrose,
turning to the wife of a member of the
House, 'what time the division is expected to be taken ?'

'Not until the small hours, I believe,'
was the reply.

'So, you see,' said our hostess, 'we
shall go to bed without knowing what
has happened.'

'I cannot understand myself,' said Canon Caryl, 'the absorbing interest in politics, which so many find. My poor brother Charles, whom you remember, used to tell me how, after the great division in 1832, almost worn out with fatigue and exhaustion, he walked, in broad daylight, up to the gate in the Green Park in Piccadilly, towards his lodgings in Bury Street, and chanced upon an early milkman. He said the most delightful draught he ever took, was the glass of milk he drank then, fresh from the scene of excitement and turmoil, and hoarse from cheering, though he gave a silent vote himself,—" And the milkman," he used to add, " had no idea that the constitution of society, and of all classes, including his own, in England, had been changed by a Parliamentary vote, an hour before."'

'It is the milkman you speak of,' said Miss de Chamier, 'whom Mr Eardley would not enfranchise. As a Liberal, he would educate the milkman to understand public questions, before he trusted him to give a vote upon them.'

'It would take a long time,' I ventured to observe, 'to make the lower classes look at politics, even when they take any interest in them, except from the point of personal concern,—of rates and taxes,—of beer or no beer, as the case may be; and their vote, when they get it, will be for the man who promises most.'

Canon Caryl laughed silently, as the ladies went upstairs.

'You want to change and reform human nature, before you extend the franchise and, in theory, as a Catholic, I agree. But this country is rapidly growing democratic, and you, as you are young, will live to see changes in that direction, which now seem impossible. If the greatness of this country is to last, as I believe it will, it will be the high-mindedness and un-deviating principle of great statesmen,—of individuals, who will maintain it, and who will stem the torrent which is already swelling; and I am glad to see a Radical like Eardley sacrificing much to his love of truth, for, after all, even if he obtain office in another Ministry, to break with his party is always a terrible struggle to an honest, patriotic man.'

The next morning the newspapers were eagerly read. The division had gone against the Government. Eardley had made a most eloquent and closely-reas-oned speech, which had at once estab-lished his fame as an orator. There was no doubt the Government would resign. I hurried up after breakfast to Devonshire

Place, where I found my dear friend in raptures over Eardley's classical description of the modern democrat, with his crude ideas and his reckless theories, and his contempt for all the lessons of history and philosophy.

Reading these grand periods, and at this eventful epoch of English Parliamentary life, her and my thoughts were with dear William, who was still in bed! He must get into Parliament, if there was a General Election; and Eardley would now be a great man. The time had come; and the old lady, overjoyed, gave me a fond maternal kiss, as I hurried off to hear the latest result of the morning's news, which proved to be that the Prime Minister had left at mid-day for Windsor.

END OF VOL. I.

COLSTON AND COMPANY, PRINTERS, EDINBURGH.

www.ingramcontent.com/pod-product-compliance
Lightning Source LLC
Chambersburg PA
CBHW020111030726

47498CB00006B/2055